THE CHRISTMAS CORONER

THE CHRISTMAS CORONER

A FENWAY STEVENSON MYSTERY NOVELLA

PAUL AUSTIN ARDOIN

ISBN 978-1-949082-43-2
First Edition: October 2022

For information please visit:
www.paulaustinardoin.com

Edited by Jess Reynolds

Cover design by Ziad Ezzat of Feral Creative Colony
www.feralcreativecolony.com

10 9 8 7 6 5 4 3 2 1

TABLE OF CONTENTS

AUTHOR'S NOTE

This story takes place between the events of *The Courtroom Coroner* (Book Five of *The Fenway Stevenson Mysteries*) and *The Watchful Coroner* (Book Six).

PART 1

THREE DAYS BEFORE CHRISTMAS

CHAPTER ONE

Fenway Stevenson knocked underneath the Christmas wreath hung on the door of Craig McVie's apartment, then took a step back and looked to her right. A line of white lights dotted the railing all the way to the stairway. Elegant; not overly bright. She rubbed her hands in the cold, gray morning; the wind blew off the ocean into the apartment complex, the spaces between the buildings funneling the rushing air. Fenway stood on his welcome mat and shivered.

The door swung open. McVie stood in the tiled entry in his undershirt and black uniform trousers. "Sorry," he said, turning and hurrying down the hallway to his bedroom. "I'm just about ready."

Fenway stepped into the apartment. The room still had a faint scent of Douglas fir; the festive, slim Christmas tree in the corner glowed with warm white lights. "I thought it was your night with Megan yesterday, Craig," Fenway said, putting the fingerprint kit on the side table and leaning her five-ten form against the wall.

"I lost her to *Legends of a Frozen Earth*," McVie grunted, pulling on his long-sleeved black Dominguez County Sheriff's Office shirt.

"Playing online with her friends sounded better than hanging out with her dad."

Fenway nodded, trying to look as sympathetic as possible—the new SonicSlate gaming system had been sold out for weeks. Amy had one; McVie didn't.

He buttoned his shirt hastily. "Now let's get out of here—I don't want to keep Jack Dragon waiting."

Fenway looked at McVie blankly. "You mentioned him on the phone—should I know who he is?"

"He's been the anchor for the Channel 12 news for, I don't know, five years now?" McVie said. "I know you've seen him. He announced your win in the coroner election. And I have the news on sometimes when you stay over." He coughed. "Speaking of which, don't you think it's time you got a key to my place?"

Fenway's stomach dropped, and her shoulders tensed. "I'm not usually paying attention to the news when I spend the night."

"Don't change the subject. You know the key is practical more than anything. You've got a drawer here—one in the bathroom, too. If you ever leave anything over here by accident, you can get it without—"

"I don't have anything else here, though—everything's at my place. My mom's paintings on the wall. My coffeemaker. The stack of books on my bedside table."

"I have a coffeemaker. You could leave books over here, too. I'll take you to the library. You can get all the books you want."

The library—Fenway hadn't been inside a public library since she'd moved from Seattle. Her mother used to take her all the time. One summer, she was obsessed with mystical creatures, mostly unicorns and griffins, and there had been a book she'd checked out four or five times. Fenway blinked; she remembered it had a long, pedantic title. *The Life and Times of Amazing Beasts.* No, that wasn't it, but it was something similar—

"Fenway?"

She snapped her head up. "What?"

"I asked you if you had any other concerns about taking—"

"It hasn't even been two months since we officially started dating." Fenway unzipped her jacket halfway in McVie's warm kitchen. "It's too early for a drawer, let alone a key."

"I'm not talking about timing. I'm talking about practicality."

Fenway opened her mouth to say something, but she decided against it. Ever since McVie had told her he loved her, Fenway had avoided the subject. He had said it in the chaos of the courtroom a few weeks before. Had he really meant it?

It was true that Fenway had spent several nights at McVie's apartment—definitely not *most* nights, as McVie had spent some at her place too. And it was true that she had forgotten her regular work shoes at home one night, but she was able to make it back to her apartment to get appropriate footwear rather than show up for work in tennis shoes.

"Besides," McVie continued, grinning, "calling it 'only two months' is misleading at best. It's not like we just met."

Fenway ran a hand over her face and gave McVie a slow smile. "I still think it's too soon. Although maybe I can be convinced to get a key. You've got some nice stuff I can sell online."

"The comedy stylings of Fenway Stevenson, everyone. Tip your waitstaff."

Fenway narrowed her eyes. "Have you told Amy about us yet?"

"No."

"Why not?"

"When would I have said anything? At her wedding? It would've looked like sour grapes."

"It's been three weeks since the wedding."

McVie shrugged. "They just got back from the honeymoon. I haven't—look, I just haven't wanted to talk to her, okay?"

Fenway stopped for a moment. Why was it so important to her that Amy know? "Yeah—I guess I wanted her to find out from you directly. I thought it would be easier that way."

McVie's face went blank. "Yeah, I'll bring it up with her. Next time I see her." He bent down and tied his shoes, pulling the black laces tight, then sprang to his feet. Even though he was nearly a decade and a half older than Fenway, he looked younger than his forty-three years: a boyish grin played on his lips, and in his uniform, he looked strong, lithe, and muscular.

He reached into his pocket and pulled out a single key. "Just take it. Then you can come back and get your shoes whenever you want."

"Let's talk about it later," Fenway said, breathing in his scent as he walked past her out the door, a hint of leather and cardamom tickling her nose. "Besides, you don't know me that well. I could be a serial killer." She followed him.

"Lock up, would you?" McVie said. "Oh, wait, you can't—you don't have a key."

Fenway rolled her eyes as McVie reached around her and locked the deadbolt.

They rode in silence in McVie's beige Toyota Highlander. In the gray light of the morning, a few houses they passed still had their Christmas lights turned on, some in bright reds and greens, some all in white. As they took the on-ramp to Ocean Highway, an SUV with antlers on the hood passed them, traveling at least twenty miles an hour over the speed limit. Fenway stared out the window as they passed a billboard advertising a holiday sale at the auto mall.

"Have you talked to Charlotte yet?" McVie said.

"Yeah, but she hasn't made any decisions. I think she'll wind up spending Christmas with her parents in Laguna Beach."

"Might be the best thing for her."

Fenway opened her mouth to say something, then closed it. She'd hated her stepmother for over a decade, but now that her dad was in a coma, Fenway had seen how devoted Charlotte had been. She visited the hospital every day and stayed for hours. Fenway grudgingly had to admit that Charlotte wasn't the gold digger Fenway had thought.

They took the exit for Route 326. After a couple of miles, the road twisted through the state park, then McVie turned right when his phone instructed him. A winding road took them up a hill, tall ironwoods and a few redwoods lining both sides of the lane.

After several minutes, the road ended at a cross street, and McVie slowed at the stop sign. There was no cross traffic nor street signs. She glanced at McVie; it wasn't like him not to use his turn signal.

Then McVie was driving across the intersection onto a gravel road that pitched steeply downhill. Fenway gasped.

"What was that?" McVie asked.

"What?"

"You made a noise."

"Maybe I did. I thought you were driving us off a cliff." Fenway peered out the window to look at the trees, which blocked the view all the way around. "Is this still Dominguez County?"

"According to the map, there's another four miles to the county line."

"Your destination," said the phone's pleasing female robot voice, "is on the left in five hundred feet."

"See? This isn't even far enough into the woods to hide a body." McVie braked lightly, then turned the steering wheel hard to the left. Fenway hadn't even seen the break in the trees where a driveway snaked its tongue out to meet the gravel road.

The house—a log cabin—was small and square, sitting in a clearing at the end of the driveway. Five wooden steps led to a wrap-around porch. The only holiday decoration was a tasteful pine wreath with silver ribbon hung on the front door.

A covered carport stood to the left of the house, elevated slightly, and a sleek red sports car sat in the center of the two-car space. At the side of the carport closest to the log cabin sat a gold Lexus sedan, its tires and undercarriage covered with mud. A police cruiser was parked in a gravel area on the far side of the carport.

"Who called this in?" Fenway asked.

"Deputy Salvador. She was the closest patrol officer at the time. But I bet she's at her wit's end with Jack Dragon."

"No," Fenway mused, "Celeste isn't the type to get all moony over local celebrities."

McVie chuckled. "That's not what I meant."

They got out of the Highlander and walked up the five steps to the porch. Fenway heard Celeste's fake laugh coming from inside. McVie reached out a fist and knocked loudly on the door.

A Filipina woman of medium height, wearing a beige county deputy uniform, opened the door almost immediately. "Sheriff! Coroner! You're here!"

"We can take over, Deputy Salvador," McVie said.

Celeste mouthed "thank you," then cleared her throat, opening the door farther.

A white man sat on the sofa in the living room, his back to the door. He had a photo album open on his lap. His salt-and-pepper hair was cut short, and his dark brown suit showed about a quarter inch of his goldenrod shirt collar.

"I secured the house," said Salvador. "No one but Mr. Dragon and the deceased on the premises." She took out her notebook. "Driver's license is of a Victoria Versini. Seems to be the right height and weight."

"The right height and weight?" Fenway asked, then she grimaced. "Oh—that would mean—"

"A lot of, uh, facial damage. No weapon found so far, but the victim looks to have been killed by a single twelve-gauge shotgun blast." Celeste motioned with her head toward the bedroom. "Her body's in there."

"Possible suicide?"

"It doesn't look like it to me, but I'm not the coroner." She ran her tongue over her teeth. "It's pretty grim."

Fenway set her mouth in a line and motioned to the man on the sofa. "And where was this—uh, journalist?"

"Mr. Dragon came here at six thirty to pick up Ms. Versini for their rehearsal."

"Rehearsal?" Fenway shot a questioning look at Salvador.

"Jack Dragon has hosted the TV coverage of the Estancia Christmas Day Parade since he started at Channel 12," McVie said.

"This is year six," Dragon called from the sofa. "It's quite wonderful to have such a show to put on annually."

"I believe Channel 12 is having—uh, *was* having—Victoria Versini co-host this year?" McVie raised his voice slightly.

"That's right," Jack Dragon said tersely. "She posts pretty pictures of ghastly recipes on her Photoxio—suddenly *she's* the huge star, lording her thousands of followers over us. She said the phrase 'traditional media' as if she'd just stepped in dog shit." Dragon turned and smiled, showcasing two bright-white rows of perfectly straight teeth. "Good and bad, of course. We expected huge ratings because of her, so the budget went up. Nancy and I got our limousines back. Nicer trailers, too."

Fenway nodded and turned back toward the bedroom. McVie came up next to her. "Do you know who this Victoria Versini is?"

"Sure," Fenway replied. "You know how I love weird recipes."

"I figured this would be up your alley."

"Interesting food combinations for sure. And the photography always made the dishes look so good. Whoever did her photography deserves a raise."

"You were a fan?"

"Absolutely not," Fenway said. "I tried the recipes. Uniformly terrible. Or worse, bland."

McVie elbowed her lightly in the ribs. "You sure it wasn't an issue with the chef?"

"Quite sure," Fenway said, trying not to smile at McVie's attempt at levity. "On that, Mr. Dragon and I agree: the recipes are ghastly." She glanced over her shoulder at Dragon, still sitting on the sofa. "He seems to be taking it well. And he obviously didn't like her much."

"You know how it is with people who work in the news. They get desensitized to everything."

"Even a woman's face getting blown off by a shotgun?"

"He's probably seen a lot worse."

"In photos. Video footage. It's different when it's right in front of you."

"Maybe." McVie paused. "I'll talk to him, see where he was last night."

"Need anything else here?" Salvador said.

McVie shook his head. "You can go. I'll let you know if I have any more questions."

Fenway looked around the cabin as Deputy Salvador exited through the front door. The room smelled of pine and oak, rubbing oil, and a faint hint of burning marshmallows. Reds and greens were the dominant colors; the logs of the cabin walls gave a golden-brown hue to everything inside. Fenway recognized some artwork in the style of the local Chumash tribes on the walls. She frowned. "Was this Miss Versini's house?"

"What?" Dragon said, craning his neck from his spot on the sofa. "Oh, no. The cabin belongs to Hank and Tricia."

"Hank and Tricia?"

"Henry and Patricia Rampart," Dragon said. "Henry's the one who discovered Miss Versini, after all."

"If Henry discovered her, why aren't we talking to him?"

"Oh—no, Henry didn't discover the body," McVie said. "He made Versini a star."

"Not to have her tell it," Dragon said, a twinkle in his eye. "But it's his media company that owns the rights to most of the photography. He does a lot with artists to get them noticed, make them money."

"Kind of a super-agent," Fenway ventured.

"Yes, exactly," Dragon mused, standing and turning to face McVie and Fenway. "Makes me think I should hire him to manage *my* career."

"And—what, the Ramparts just let Victoria stay here?"

"Well, at least for the Christmas parade, yes," Dragon said. "I've been picking her up for rehearsals all week."

"So you saw her yesterday?"

"Of course." Dragon sniffed. "This is a bit out of my way, but I don't mind."

"Is that your Lexus in the carport?"

Dragon raised his eyebrows. "That's correct."

"What time did you arrive yesterday?" Fenway asked.

"Six thirty."

"That seems early."

"The parade starts at nine o'clock Christmas morning. Might as well get used to the schedule." Dragon tapped his chin. "I believe Victoria had just finished posting one of her famous Photoxio videos. She talked my ear off in the car about a new recipe and a new local provider of vegetables—asparagus or arugula or something like that."

"You don't remember what it was?"

Jack sighed and examined his fingernails. "All that woman does —er, *did*—was talk my ear off. She expected everyone to be just as into her recipes as she was." He looked up at Fenway, then glanced at McVie. "Don't get me wrong—I loved that she was getting the public more interested in the parade. Having our trailers back is wonderful." Dragon smiled. "She had an inflated sense of self-worth."

McVie chuckled. "I bet you see that all the time in your line of work."

"In some people, it's charming," Dragon said. "In others, it's infuriating."

"And which one was she?"

Dragon steepled his hands and stared at them, his eyes losing focus. "Neither. She's all sizzle and no steak, and if you have the grill on long enough, you start tuning out the sizzle after a while."

Fenway nodded. "She had her own car here, didn't she? Why did you drive her to rehearsals?"

Dragon rolled his eyes. "Her car is too precious to leave in a public lot, or some such nonsense. As if this town isn't crawling with enough of those overpriced sports cars as it is." He pursed his lips, and his tone softened. "I offered, however, because I wanted to get to know her. Or more precisely, I wanted to *learn* from her."

"Hmm," Fenway mumbled.

Dragon tilted his head with a smirk. "I know that judgmental look, Coroner," he said. "This old dog can be taught new tricks. I wanted to keep that trailer and keep my paycheck, and I didn't want to rely on the mercurial Victoria Versini to do so."

"I see," Fenway replied. "Did you drive her home yesterday, too?"

"Yes. I dropped her off around eight o'clock. She said she had to work on a blog post."

"And then where did you go?"

Dragon thought. "Let me see. Victoria and I discussed getting dinner, but she wanted to get back quickly. So I—" He shook his head. "No. I thought about getting some takeout, but instead I went home. I knew I'd have to be up early for rehearsals today, so I cooked a simple meal for myself at home and went to bed."

"Did anyone see you?"

He gave Fenway a wide smile that didn't reach his eyes. "I fear I've been living the life of a bachelor ever since the former Mrs. Dragon asked for my hand in divorce years ago."

Fenway pressed her lips together.

"Had I known Miss Versini would meet an untimely end," Dragon continued, "I would have made sure to have an alibi."

Fenway cocked her head. What an odd way to phrase that. Maybe.

"How did Henry Rampart meet Miss Versini?" McVie said, pulling out a notebook.

Dragon hesitated.

"What is it?" McVie said.

"Well—one mustn't spread rumors."

"Rumors?"

Dragon stroked his chin and clicked his tongue. "Honestly, it's pure conjecture on my part. I always see them together, that's all. The three of them. Perhaps she's like a surrogate daughter to them." His eyes darted to Fenway. "I don't like to speak of my suspicions in mixed company."

Ah. Jack Dragon obviously thought the Ramparts were in some sort of romantic relationship with Versini. She blinked hard to stop herself from rolling her eyes.

McVie turned to Fenway and lowered his voice. "I can take care of questioning Mr. Dragon."

"What?" Fenway whispered. "Are you afraid you'll offend my delicate sensibilities?"

"I'm afraid Mr. Dragon will censor himself with you here. Besides, shouldn't you get started on the physical evidence?"

Jack Dragon was a fascinating character, but Fenway did have a dead body to attend to. "Just need to get my booties on." She slipped on her plastic overshoes, then stepped through the doorway on her left into the bedroom.

The huge bedroom was more subdued in its color palette than the living room, though it had a country design to it. The earth tones, silver, and yellow reminded Fenway of the inside of a barn—or at least what barns looked like on TV.

The king-size bed was positioned with its headboard against the inside wall; about four feet of space separated the foot of the bed from a large Queen Anne-style desk.

Upon the desk rested a laptop, its lid at a thirty-degree angle, nearer to closed than open.

The framed picture on the wall behind the desk, a towering print of a Joan Miró, looked out of place in the room. Its glass was pockmarked with nicks and holes from, Fenway assumed, the shotgun pellets. Sitting in the desk chair, turned to face the bed, was the corpse, dressed in stylish red pajamas with white piping under a charcoal-gray brushed terry cloth robe that was splayed open.

There was a lot of blood, and yes, Celeste had been accurate: the shotgun blast had been close to Versini's head. Enough where prints or DNA would have to provide the concrete identification.

Although Fenway had a strong stomach, she was glad she hadn't eaten yet. She set the medical kit on the floor, took her phone out, and called the CSI team in San Miguelito.

CHAPTER TWO

PUTTING HER PHONE ON CAMERA MODE, FENWAY TOOK PICTURES of Victoria Versini's body. The dead woman was seated, her torso pressed against the back of the chair, her head lolling back. Blood had spattered in all directions: the coverlet on the bed was spotted with red, and so was the hardwood floor. But Fenway noticed a triangular area next to the bed that was free of blood spatter.

"The killer stood right there," she mumbled. Melissa de la Garza might be able to provide some more information once she analyzed the scene, maybe even about the height or size of the killer.

She knelt in a clean spot next to the body and put her hand on the dead woman's shoulder—

And the room began to spin.

Fenway shut her eyes.

Her father lay on the floor, face up.

A wound in his upper chest, on the left side, just below his shoulder.
Before Fenway's eyes, the bloom of blood on his white dress shirt grew from a carnation to a rose to a lily.

Nathaniel Ferris had leaped in front of her and taken the bullet.

"Help!" she cried, tearing her gray blazer off and putting it over the wound, both hands down, all her weight on it. "Help! My dad's been shot!"

Despite the motion all around her, she concentrated on the blood, warm and wet, soaking through the jacket.

She opened her eyes. Deep breaths. She counted to ten on an inhale, and the room slowly spun to a stop.

Maybe she'd leave the body alone for a moment. Get her bearings.

There was still a lot to do in here, after all.

Fenway chose a clean corner of the room to set up her medical kit. She put on a pair of gloves and dusted the door handles and all the surfaces in the room that weren't covered with blood. There were a few prints on the top of the headboard and on the snooze button of the alarm clock, but none on the door handle. Fenway suspected the killer had wiped the handle clean after the fact. Good chance that no gloves were worn, which meant there was a possibility of the killer leaving fingerprints *somewhere*.

A small black canvas equipment bag was next to the bed, on the other side from the doorway, and Fenway unzipped it slowly. She found three individual cases inside the bag and carefully opened each: a small USB camera, a tripod, and a ring light—all clean, with no blood or detritus on anything. Fenway zipped up the bag. The canvas was too uneven to get prints, and the camera, tripod, and light seemed like they'd been in their cases. Can't be too thorough, of course, but Fenway mentally moved the equipment down her priority list to fingerprint.

Fenway heard the door open and close, then outside, the sound of a car starting and driving away. She walked out into the kitchen, where McVie stood leaning against the counter, his chin in his hand, lost in thought.

"You don't think it was Jack Dragon?"

McVie shook his head. "I poked my head in there while you were fingerprinting the bedside table. You saw the area next to the bed where there was no blood on the floor?"

Fenway nodded. "I think that's where the killer stood."

"Me too," McVie said, "and unless Mr. Dragon had another gaudy five-thousand-dollar suit hidden in the closet, it wasn't him. He had a little blood on the sole of his shoe, and when he found the stain, you would have thought *he* was the one who'd been shot."

Fenway smiled.

"Anyway, no, I don't think it was him." He pushed himself upright. "You have a time of death?"

Fenway grimaced. "I—I didn't think I should touch the blood spatter before CSI gets here."

"So no liver temp."

"No."

"Any rigor mortis?"

"Uh, I haven't checked yet. I wanted to get prints first."

"The sooner you check the body, the more accurate your time-of-death estimate will be."

"True." Fenway licked her lips cautiously. "But I can't check for rigor without disturbing the bloodstains."

McVie smiled. "Don't tell me you were making excuses not to touch the body. You were grossed out?"

"I was not." Fenway swallowed hard. "I was being careful of the forensic evidence. Besides, *you're* one to talk."

McVie paused for a moment—did he suspect the reason Fenway hadn't touched the body yet?—then a gentle smile came over his face. "I freely admit you have a stronger stomach than I do. I think your love for lengua tacos proves that."

"Okay, then." Fenway turned to the spray of blood on the floor and was relieved the room stayed still. "Based on how dry the bloodstains are, I'm sure it's been at least two or three hours. Probably more."

"Did you get prints?"

"Some. None on the door handle, though."

"Maybe the door was open when the killer came in."

Fenway shook her head. "No prints at all. I'm pretty sure the handle was wiped clean."

"Oh," McVie said. "Front door?"

"We'll get Jack Dragon's prints, and probably Deputy Salvador's, and maybe even yours. But I bet that was also wiped clean when the killer was leaving. If things were wiped, that suggests that the killer didn't wear gloves."

"Interesting."

Fenway pressed her lips together. "It's a working theory," she said. "I'll print the front door to make sure." She walked into the bedroom and came out with the kit, setting it next to the front door and brushing the doorknob.

"You'll do the outside too, right?"

"Yes, mother dearest," Fenway said, batting her eyelashes with a coquettish fervor she didn't quite feel. "Then can I play video games for an hour before bed?"

"But no caffeine." McVie chuckled. "I'll start making a list of Miss Versini's colleagues and friends."

"Start with Hank and Tricia," Fenway said. "They let her take this cabin for a week, and this close to Christmas, that suggests an unusual relationship."

"It might be nothing," McVie said. "Maybe her family isn't around. It's strange to work on Christmas when you don't need to—unless you don't have anywhere else to go." McVie set his jaw, and a shadow fell over his face.

"This year sucks for both of us, doesn't it?" Fenway said quietly.

McVie scoffed. "You can say that again. It'll be weird being a stranger in Amy's house."

"At least you'll be with your daughter," Fenway said. "Hopefully time with Megan will cancel the bad blood with your ex."

McVie nodded. "I'd invite you along, Fenway, but it's going to be awkward enough—"

"No offense, but Christmas with my boyfriend's ex-wife isn't my idea of a great holiday. I guess you're right. It's not a good time to announce that we're dating."

"Are you and Charlotte going to spend Christmas together?"

"I don't know yet. She invited me. Probably wants to get some takeout while we cry over Dad being in the hospital." She peeled off the fingerprint tape and transferred it to a card. "But I'll be working anyway. Who knows? This case probably won't be closed by then."

"I can work Christmas too."

Fenway shook her head. "You don't have to do that."

"I know, but what else am I going to do? Watch basketball and movie reruns in the apartment by myself before going over to Amy's?" He shook his head. "I just know it'll be two hours of looking at their honeymoon pictures while they make not-so-veiled references to how rich they are."

"I could tell you how rich my father is if it'll make you feel better." A flash of her father's body on the floor of the courtroom, but Fenway blinked and it was gone.

McVie laughed. "Yeah. I'll lord that over her. 'Your husband might be rich, but he'll never be as rich as my new girlfriend's dad!'"

"That would be just the right amount of awkward and crazy." Fenway opened the door and brushed fingerprint dust on the outside handle, then bent down to examine it. "Just like I thought, by the way. Four prints on the inside doorknob. In the right place for a thumb and forefinger, too. Probably two of Jack Dragon's and two of Deputy Salvador's. The outside should have Jack Dragon's, and maybe that's it."

"Or maybe the killer only wiped off the inside."

"Ever the optimist, Craig." She peered at the outside door handle. "That's a nice, fat, juicy thumbprint if I've ever seen one. And at first glance, it matches the one on the inside. That'll be Mr. Dragon's, I bet. Don't suppose you got his prints before he left."

McVie pointed to the mug on the counter. "He found some Earl Gray in the cabinet while he was waiting for us. You might find another print or two on the electric kettle next to the sink."

Fenway transferred the tape to another card, then stood and smiled. "You think of everything."

"I do okay," McVie said.

Fenway dusted the mug, and sure enough, two of those prints matched the ones on the door. The other two could almost certainly be matched to Deputy Salvador, as they had seen her open the door when they walked in.

The CSI van arrived just as Fenway closed the fingerprint kit, and moments later, Melissa de la Garza walked through the open door in booties and coveralls, her curly black hair tucked into a cap, a kit in one hand and a camera bag in the other.

"Through there?" she said. "Is it bad?"

Fenway shifted her weight from foot to foot. "I saw worse in my forensics classes. I've taken prints of everything that didn't have blood all over it."

"You—you took prints?"

"Yes," Fenway said, feeling the color rise to her face. She should have checked for rigor; she should have gotten the liver temp. She should have pushed through.

"Did you get the liver—"

"No," Fenway said quickly. "I didn't touch the body. I didn't want to mess up the blood spatter."

"Shotgun from close range, the blood spatter won't tell us very much," Melissa said.

"I didn't know that. Figured it was better safe than sorry."

Melissa narrowed her eyes, but not unkindly. "Are you okay?"

Fenway cleared her throat and nodded. "Sure."

Melissa nodded, but Fenway saw in her eyes that Melissa wasn't convinced.

They walked into the bedroom. Melissa took out a camera and took several dozen photographs of the scene.

She put the camera away and glanced up at Fenway. "You ever done a liver temp before?"

Fenway shook her head. "Not lately."

"No? Well, that's all right. Now's your chance."

"Let me find me find my thermometer."

Fenway looked up to see Melissa holding out both a sharp probe and the thermometer, the spike hanging from a thick cord like undercooked spaghetti.

"Thanks." Fenway took the probe and the thermometer. She breathed in, counted to ten, exhaled. The room didn't spin.

Despite the spate of murders that had swept Estancia over the last six months, Fenway hadn't taken the temperature of a corpse since her crime scene class at Seattle University perhaps a year earlier. She walked to the body and leaned over, setting the thermometer down and holding the probe tightly in her right hand. "Like riding a bike," she murmured. A flash of the bloom of red on her father's shirt, but then it was thankfully gone. She pulled Victoria Versini's pajama top above her sternum and ran her gloved finger along the ridge. She eyeballed an inch to her left and an inch below the edge of the bone, and firmly stuck the probe in until the resistance changed, then pulled it out.

"Sharpie?" Fenway asked.

Melissa stepped over to Fenway, uncapping a red marker and handing it to her. Fenway took it and drew a circle around the hole from the probe.

"Good," Melissa said. "They taught you to distinguish the mark so it's not confused with evidence."

"It was an expensive master's program," Fenway muttered, a smile touching the corners of her mouth. "Glad I got my money's worth." She inserted the thermometer's spike into the hole.

"Eighty-six point two," Melissa read.

"About—oh—seven or eight hours," Fenway said. "I told McVie two or three hours. I thought the blood hadn't dried enough."

Melissa stepped forward and looked at the blood on the floor.

"It's dry, Fenway—a little tacky still, but dry. Longer than three hours, for sure."

"I guess I'm off my game." Fenway removed the thermometer.

"Have you found the shotgun or any shells in the room?"

Fenway shook her head. "I've searched, but not everywhere. I have a feeling the killer picked them up, but you never know—they could have gotten wedged under something. McVie's looking through the rest of the cabin."

Melissa nodded. "Shells can eject with a lot of force. I've found shotgun shells pretty far away. Behind dressers. Once in a loft twelve feet off the floor." She walked around the desk. "CSI should be ready to take her to San Miguelito in about an hour." Melissa motioned with her head out the door. "If you want to get moving on the investigation part, I can finish up here."

"Thanks, Melissa." Fenway stood and took two steps toward the door before turning her head. "By the way, are you and Deputy Huke still dating?"

Melissa suppressed a grin. "He and I are driving down to El Centro to have Christmas with my crazy parents and all the aunts and uncles tomorrow."

"Oh, meeting the family? This sounds serious."

Melissa turned back to the body and bit her lip.

Fenway's eyes went wide. "It *is* serious. Wow, you and the most uptight man I've ever met in my life—I'd never have pictured the two of you together."

"My apartment lease runs out at the end of the month," Melissa mumbled. "We're—uh—we're figuring things out."

"Has it even been six months?"

"A little over four. It's moving a little fast."

Fenway cocked her head. "But you like him?"

Melissa exhaled loudly. "Can we not discuss this over a dead body?"

Fenway shrugged. "It's really the only time you and I ever talk."

"Let's get drinks at Winfrey's after I come back next week. Right now, I've got a job to do, and I don't need pressure about moving in with Donny when I'm working."

Fenway tried not to let the grin slide over her face as she walked out of the bedroom.

CHAPTER THREE

McVie and Fenway left the cabin after another twenty minutes when an M.E. assistant arrived to help Melissa with the body. Fenway called Deputy Salvador to find relatives of Victoria Versini for next-of-kin notification. She hung up as she got into McVie's passenger seat.

"What now?"

McVie squinted and started the engine, backing out of the driveway. "You know, I'm only sheriff for another week and a half, and you're going to have to learn how to take more of a leadership role in these investigations."

Fenway narrowed her eyes at McVie. "I think I've done all right for myself."

"Sure," McVie said quickly, driving down the gravel road the way they'd come. "But come January first, I won't be around for you to ask, 'what now?' Don't get me wrong; Gretchen—uh, Sheriff Donnelly—is great, but she's more of a people manager than an investigator. You ask her what to do in a murder investigation and she'll break out a procedure manual."

"That's funny; Dez thinks we should be a little more procedure-oriented in our investigations."

"Oh, she does? That's not just a criticism of my management style?"

"It could be both." Fenway grinned.

"Yeah, okay, whatever."

"Whatever yourself, short-timer." She cleared her throat. "We said the first order of business was interviewing the owners of the cabin. At the very least, we should make sure they aren't being targeted."

"Right. Hank and Tricia Rampart."

"They might have gone out of town. It's the holidays, after all."

"Maybe." McVie rubbed his chin thoughtfully. "Jack Dragon said they were close to our victim. Obviously, he thinks there's more to it than that—he almost hit me over the head with his double entendres."

"Yeah," Fenway said slowly, "but he's a news anchor looking for a good story, isn't he? We can't take what he says seriously."

"I don't know," McVie said, scratching his temple with his index finger. "He was supposedly a big deal in one of the larger markets— Phoenix, I think. Moved to the coast to take things a little easier after a health scare."

"Where did you hear that?"

"An interview he did a couple of years ago."

"We'll see." Fenway pulled her phone out of her purse and called Dez, who gave Fenway the Ramparts' home address, a small bungalow near downtown Estancia, as well as their places of business. "What do you think, Craig? Three days before Saint Nick comes down the chimney—are the Ramparts more likely at home or work?"

"The sheriff's office isn't too far away from the Ramparts' house," McVie said. "We'll see if they're home. If not, we'll give their offices a call. Like you said, they could be out of town."

The Ramparts' house was on Ninth Street, only about a quarter mile from the city center. The cottage was painted a bright yellow with a front door made of wide vertical wooden planks and wrought-iron hardware. The small windows on either side of the front door showcased shutters made of the same wood and iron. A string of large multi-colored bulbs stretched along the gutters at the roofline, but there were no other holiday decorations save a large green wreath with a red bow on the front door. The lawn was neat, with a raised flowerbed of pansies on the side of the house that served as a separator from the neighbors' yard. There was no driveway, but Fenway had seen houses in this neighborhood, and she suspected a standalone garage behind the house emptied into the alley between Ninth and Tenth Streets. McVie parked on the street.

"Think they're home?" he said as they walked up the narrow brick path to the front door.

"No," Fenway said. "My money's on a trip to see family back east somewhere."

"I think they *are* home," McVie said. "Care to make a little wager on it?"

"A wager?"

"Yep."

"Like what? Twenty bucks?"

McVie rolled his eyes. "So unimaginative. No. Something better than money."

"Better than money?"

"If I win, you have to take my spare key."

Fenway grinned. "If I win, you have to eat two lengua tacos at Dos Milagros next time we go."

"Oof. It has to be lengua?"

"Craig, it's *so good*. You can't keep getting the carnitas burrito there. That's like going to a fancy steak place and getting the chicken. You don't like Dos Milagros because you're not ordering the right things."

A flash of seriousness on McVie's face: *And you're not letting our relationship blossom because you're not treating us the right way, either.*

Fenway's smile faltered.

Fenway took a few steps on the sidewalk to the right until she could see around the side of the house. She was right: the driveway was in the back, a late-model Mercedes SUV parked there. She hurried to join McVie on the small porch in front of the door. Despite the rustic feel of the house's facade, a modern camera doorbell shone its cool round blue light like a futuristic sentry.

"We may not find out whether they're home or not." McVie motioned to the doorbell. "They could be in France and talk to us as if they were inside."

"If they're Schrodinger's witnesses, then no key and no lengua," Fenway said.

"Nope. I think we both lose. Key *and* tacos."

Fenway gave McVie the side-eye. "You must really want me to take that damn key. It's really only been two months, Craig."

He reached out and rang the electronic doorbell. The synthesized chime sounded on the porch as the blue light flashed and chased around in a circle.

Fenway's phone buzzed in her purse. She ignored it.

"Yes?" A man's voice sounded from the doorbell intercom.

"It's Sheriff McVie," he said, holding his badge up to the doorbell so the camera could catch it. "Are you Henry Rampart?"

"I am."

"You're the owner of a cabin at 244 Swedish Canyon Road?"

"My wife and I, yes," came the voice. "What's this about?"

"It would be easier to speak to you in person, sir," McVie said. "I'm afraid there's been an incident at your property."

"What? An incident? What kind of incident?"

"If we could come in—"

"Yes—sorry. It's the holidays. Still in my pajamas. Tricia and I will be right there."

McVie and Fenway stood at the door. He scuffled his shoes on the porch while Fenway stared straight ahead.

"Looks like I win." McVie's voice was soft.

"Congratulations."

They still hadn't talked about their feelings for each other. Fenway hated the typical "we need to have a talk" talk. McVie, to his credit, hadn't pushed Fenway to reciprocate—nor had he repeated his declaration of love to her after the day of the courtroom shooting. But he'd brought up the key once too often. She might have to take the key to make him shut up about it.

A skinny white man of medium height opened the door. His thinning black hair was disheveled, but his eyes were bright. He had a weak jawline with two or three days' worth of stubble. His green robe was of thin cloth, wrapped tightly around him against the chilly December day. His green plaid pajama pants were visible below the knee-length hem of his robe, and he wore faded brown leather slippers.

A Black woman appeared behind him. She was perhaps two or three inches shorter. Her thick bushy hair, styled in an Afro blowout, stood in sharp contrast to her husband's balding pate. She had large, deep brown eyes and a round face with full lips—even without lipstick. She carried herself with a confidence and ease that immediately made Fenway envious. There was no flicker in her eyes of questioning whether the sheriff at the door would accept them as a mixed-race couple—something Fenway still fought against whenever she and McVie went to dinner or a movie. She was the first to speak.

"I'm Tricia Rampart, and this is my husband, Hank." She held out her hand, and Fenway shook it. Tricia's hand was smooth and cool.

"Sheriff Craig McVie and my colleague, Fenway Stevenson."

"You're the coroner," Tricia said to Fenway.

"I'm afraid there was an incident at your cabin," McVie continued. "Do you know a woman named Victoria Versini?"

"What's happened to Victoria?" Hank Rampart said sharply.

"So you *do* know her," McVie said.

"She's a good friend of ours," Tricia said.

"When was the last time you saw her?"

Hank rubbed his chin. "She was here yesterday for lunch," he said, his voice wavering. "We dropped her off at the cabin afterward."

"Did she seem okay? Nervous, excited, upset—anything?"

"She was excited to get her Photoxio post up," Hank said. "Had a cup of coffee with us and chatted after we cleared the dishes away. I didn't think there was anything out of the ordinary."

"Did she post to Photoxio yesterday?" Fenway asked, scrolling through her phone.

"I—I don't know. I don't check her feed every day. I didn't yesterday. Maybe Tricia did."

Tricia nodded. "Yes. I saw it. It was a good video."

"What was it about?" Hank asked, scratching his head. "Something on one of the local vegetable farmers here, wasn't it?"

"It was a video post about heirloom artichokes."

"That *does* sound exciting," McVie murmured. Fenway bumped him with her knee.

"Did you check at the studio?" Tricia asked. "Jack Dragon was supposed to pick her up. She doesn't like to park the Spyder on the street."

"She drives an Alfa Romeo, correct?"

"Yes—a red convertible. Are you here because she's missing? I know she leaves her car at the cabin, so it looks like she's home, but she's not."

"No—" Fenway began, shooting a look at McVie.

He cleared his throat. "I'm sorry to tell you this, but Miss Versini was killed late last night."

Tricia wobbled as if she'd been struck, and Hank reached out to steady her.

"Victoria—" Tricia moaned.

"I just, uh, I just—" Hank stammered. "Was—was it a car accident?"

"I'm afraid not," McVie said.

"Perhaps we should go in and sit," Fenway suggested.

As if controlled by puppet strings, Hank turned, his hand still on Tricia's shoulder, and she cast her eyes downward. "I should make some coffee," Tricia mumbled.

McVie followed Hank and shot a glance at Fenway.

"Why don't I help?" Fenway said, a little too brightly. She placed her arm on Tricia's shoulder as Hank slouched his way into the living room.

"The kitchen is this way," Tricia said, her voice flat.

As they went through the archway into the small but cozy kitchen, Fenway glanced around. Oh no. It was a full espresso machine, all shiny stainless steel and embossed brass lettering. Fenway could barely operate the drip coffee maker she'd owned since college. Screwing up the steamed milk was guaranteed to get Tricia and her off on the wrong foot.

To Fenway's relief, Tricia pulled a black drip coffeemaker from behind the espresso machine and began filling up the carafe from the faucet. She looked up. "I just spoke to her on the phone last night."

Fenway wanted to get the notebook out of her purse, but Tricia had downturned eyes and a slightly quivering bottom lip—and she'd just let the carafe overflow without making a move to stop it. Would Tricia be more forthcoming without a reminder that this was a police interview?

"You're full," Fenway said.

"Oh," Tricia said slowly, reaching out a hand to turn the tap off.

"Are you all right?"

"I don't understand." Tricia sounded dazed, and she leaned on the counter. "She was just here. She was sitting at the table right there."

Fenway's phone dinged in her purse again, but she ignored it. "I'm so sorry for your loss," Fenway said. "You were close?"

"She was—she was like a daughter to us." Tricia glanced up at Fenway, then lifted the carafe out of the sink, pouring the excess down the drain before filling the reservoir of the coffeemaker. "She and Avery were best friends growing up, and afterward, Victoria was so good. So kind to us. And to think that her father—" She shook her head. "Sorry. It's just that they're both gone now. I don't really know what to do."

She reached out to close the top of the coffee maker, and Fenway stepped next to her, grabbing the small bag of PQCR French Roast off the counter.

"Sorry," Tricia said. "Silly of me."

Fenway smiled, opened the lid, and scooped several heaping tablespoons of coffee into the filter, then closed it. Tricia tapped the *Start* button.

Fenway gave Tricia a small, encouraging smile.

"Thank you," Tricia murmured.

"So," Fenway said gently, "after you dropped Victoria back at the cabin after lunch, take me through your day."

"Sure," Tricia said, straightening up. "On the way back, we went grocery shopping. We got back around three, and then we watched some television. Hank had a poker night with some of his friends, and I made myself some dinner, then I wrapped presents for a while. I think I was asleep by nine."

"What time did Hank come back from poker?"

"He usually gets home by eleven or so." Tricia smiled, but it didn't reach her eyes. "He and his friends sometimes think they're still in college, but I know they can't go much past ten or ten thirty." She chuckled. "I think he was playing poker more to get out of helping me wrap presents, to be honest."

"Did he win?"

Tricia paused. "There isn't anything illegal going on. They play for fun—"

Fenway held up her hand. "We're not interested in the details of the poker game. I'm asking because it might jog your memory. You know, did he wake you up by saying he won big, and then you fell right back asleep?"

Tricia shook her head.

Fenway's phone dinged a third time.

"Do you need to get that?" Tricia asked.

Fenway took her phone out and looked at the screen—a text from Melissa. She wanted a call.

"I'll be right back," Fenway said.

"Coffee's almost ready." Tricia sighed. "Victoria was so good for us."

Fenway hesitated. No—Melissa could wait.

"You know, when Avery passed," Tricia continued, "we suddenly had this big college fund and no one to spend it on. Victoria's father had left the family."

"When was this?"

Tricia frowned. "A long time ago. Victoria was just a baby. Maybe she hadn't even been born yet." She sighed. "Last I heard, he took up with a woman half his age in Houston. Victoria and her mother were struggling to make ends meet, and then when Victoria's mother was diagnosed—" Her bottom lip quivered slightly, then she took a deep breath and got ahold of herself. "Anyway, that's when Victoria moved to town—a friend of her mom's offered a couple of spare rooms in their house. Avery and Victoria met at school. They spent so much time together, you know. They were both on the tennis team. Victoria's grades weren't as good as Avery's were, so Stanford wasn't in the cards for her, but she got into Arizona A&T. Even got a scholarship."

Fenway nodded. "Sounds like she was a real comfort to you. And you to her."

"You have no idea," Tricia said. "Do you have children?"

Fenway briefly thought of McVie's daughter, to whom she'd spoken barely twenty words in the last six months. "No, ma'am, I don't."

"It changes you," Tricia said. "We couldn't have any more after Avery, and, I don't know, maybe we spoiled her, or maybe our expectations were too high. I thought Avery would be happy once she graduated from Stanford. The world would be hers for the taking, you know?"

Fenway smiled and remembered what her mother had said after Fenway had expressed disappointment that she hadn't gotten into the University of Washington: "If, five years after you graduate, you have to tell people where you went to college, then you didn't get a good education."

"But after we found Avery in the..." Tricia trailed off. "Well, Victoria was pretty much there for us all the time. She helped organize the funeral. Hank was torn up. He could barely get out of bed. I think that's why he retired early, you know."

Fenway nodded. "I know it can be hard."

"We didn't mind paying for her school," Tricia said. "Or for some of the money she needed for the computer and the camera equipment. And Hank still had some connections." She crossed her arms. "People said we were crazy to spend that kind of money on her, that she was taking advantage of us, but look what it got her. She's making more money per year than Hank did the year he retired." Tricia cleared her throat. "I'm sorry. That's maybe too much information."

"Please, there's no need to be embarrassed. It's helping me get a good picture of who Victoria—" Fenway almost said *who Victoria was*, then stopped herself just in time. "Of how Victoria helped everyone," she finished weakly.

"We're so proud of her," Tricia said quietly. "And she doesn't have anyone else. Not with her father who knows where and with her mother—well, enough about that."

"Do you know anyone who would have wanted to hurt Victoria?" Fenway asked.

A tear ran down Tricia's cheek. "I'd like to say that everyone loved Victoria and no one would ever hurt her." She stifled a sob. "Her videos and posts could be very entertaining, but she wasn't always nice with her critiques. Some of the people she criticized, I imagine, were quite angry with her."

"Do you have any names?"

Tricia furrowed her brow in thought. "I can't think of anyone off the top of my head. But it's all on her website—or on her online video channel or in her social media feeds. It's no secret whose food she doesn't like."

Fenway nodded. "Now, I have to ask this, Mrs. Rampart. Do either you or your husband own any guns?"

Tricia paled, then swallowed hard. "We have a shotgun up at the cabin," she said. "We got it after we saw some mountain lions skulking around. Didn't want anything to happen to Bosco."

As if on cue, a black dog, about a foot and a half tall with moplike fur, came barreling out of the back room and barked at Fenway.

"Roscoe?" Fenway said, crouching down. The dog stopped barking, sniffed Fenway's outstretched hand, then flopped on its back and stretched. Fenway reached out and scratched its belly. Its hair was corded, dense and woolly.

"Bosco, with a B," Tricia said, "like the chocolate syrup." She sighed. "He's not much of a guard dog, I'm afraid."

"He's just a little love bug," Fenway told Bosco, surprising herself with her voice modulation. She'd never had a dog growing up—her father didn't like the idea, and when Fenway had left with her mother to Seattle, they'd always been too poor to afford one.

Fenway stood up. "Anything else you can tell me about Victoria?"

Tricia took four mugs out of the cupboard and poured the finished coffee into each of them. "I'm just in shock," she said. "First Avery, and now..."

Fenway didn't ask to get half-and-half in her coffee. She took two of the mugs into the living room where McVie and Hank Rampart were standing, one on each side of the long coffee table.

"I'll get you the names and numbers of the others at the poker game," Hank said. "Don't you worry." He turned to Fenway and mumbled thanks as he took the mug. Fenway gave the other mug to

McVie. She nodded to him, then lifted her phone and crossed in front of him and out the front door, calling Melissa back as she did so.

"Hi, Fenway."

"Sorry," she said. "I was talking to the victim's—uh, I guess, a sort of adoptive mother."

"You said to call you if I found anything interesting."

"Oh—good. What is it? A big fat fingerprint?"

"Someone cut the brake lines in Victoria Versini's car."

CHAPTER FOUR

Fenway leaned over Sergeant Dez Roubideaux's shoulder, looking at the laptop screen. "You got into this PC all by yourself?"

"One word about teaching an old dog new tricks, Fenway—"

"No, no," Fenway said quickly. "I was just thinking you could take Piper's old job."

"They've got someone for it already. I don't know why you refuse to meet him."

"I will, I promise." Fenway straightened up. "Anything from the fingerprint database yet?"

"Deputy Salvador. There were also prints that matched the coffee mug on the door handle."

"I assume that's Jack Dragon. He may not be in the system."

Dez handed Fenway a printout. The name *Michael Jonathan Long* was printed across the top of the page, along with a perhaps decade-old mugshot of Jack Dragon with a board reading *Duval County Sheriff's Office*.

"Michael Long?"

Dez smiled. "Come on, now, rookie, you didn't expect *Jack Dragon* to be his real name, did you?"

"I guess not."

Fenway skimmed the printout. "Arrested for grand theft auto?"

Dez pointed to the year. "He was nineteen. Took his ex-girl-friend's car for a joyride." She shook her head. "Obviously not the best decision. She pressed charges."

"You read the file?"

Dez shrugged. "More interesting than reading up on all the local produce farmers who've been pissed off by Victoria Versini's bad reviews. You've seen one angry Photoxio comment, you've seen them all."

Fenway ran her hands through her hair and scratched her scalp. "Versini's Photoxio page—and her videos—they were popular, right? So a review—good or bad—could either make or break the local farmers."

Dez harrumphed. "Not all of us buy our vegetables based on a crazy white girl's recommendation. Victoria Versini wouldn't know a spice if it up and bit her on the ass."

"I think you'll agree, Dez—you're not 'most people.'"

"And proud of it."

"Despite the depths of boredom your taste buds must sink to, we need to figure out who Versini criticized in the last few months. One of those produce people might be the culprit."

Dez grunted. "It'd be faster if we split the work."

Fenway gestured to Miguel Castaneda three desks away. "You busy, Migs?"

"I've got work to do, but if you need something, I can take it on."

"Great—can you search the legal database to see if any of the people Victoria Versini criticized began litigation against her? Filed any libel or defamation cases?"

"Sure."

Fenway turned to the screen and caught a glimpse of a Photoxio picture—this one with a comment from Victoria Versini. "Hang on, Dez."

"What?"

"That last comment—when was it made?"

Dez blinked. "This morning—about an hour ago." She looked up at Fenway. "Photoxio lets you schedule posts and comments, though. She probably set it up before last night, especially if she knew she'd be away for a few days."

Fenway leaned over the screen and pointed at the comment above. "It's a reply to another comment that was made this morning, too. I don't think it was pre-scheduled." She straightened up. "Can you see if Versini has an assistant who's posting for her? If we can talk to someone who worked for her, maybe we can ask if any of Victoria's targets have been especially argumentative."

"I'll see what I can do. The laptop would be the best source of information, but it's shot to hell."

"The Ramparts might know. Or her phone provider might be persuaded to release call logs—if Versini had an assistant, I bet we'll find dozens of calls or texts."

"I'm on it," Dez said.

"One more thing—Tricia Rampart said they kept a shotgun at the cabin, but we didn't find a shotgun there."

"You think the killer took it?"

"Or hid it. Can you find out what type of gun the Ramparts have?"

"Sure. It's better than reading Photoxio comments and trying to stop myself from tearing my hair out."

Fenway's phone rang. Charlotte. "I have to take this—thanks, Dez." She walked to her office, answering as she went. "Hi, Charlotte."

Silence on the other end of the phone.

"Charlotte, are you there?"

A sniffle. "Yes. Sorry. Hello, Fenway. I—I just wondered if you'd given any more thought to my message."

"Right. Christmas." Fenway shut her office door and plopped down in the leather task chair behind her desk. "I was surprised you invited me, frankly. I figured you'd go to Laguna Beach to have Christmas with your mom."

"I don't think I'll go this year," Charlotte said vaguely. "Thanksgiving was—well—not the greatest."

"You were really looking forward to going, weren't you?"

"Not anymore," Charlotte said.

"Did something happen?"

"I just don't like being that far away from your father."

Fenway slumped in her seat. She'd been to visit Nathaniel Ferris in the care facility every day, but she hadn't gone yet today. Charlotte needed the break—but he was still unconscious. "You know I'll go in and see him on Christmas Day. You can go to Laguna Beach if you want."

"You have your own situation to worry about."

"What, with Craig?" Fenway chortled. "He's going to spend Christmas with his daughter, his ex, and her new rich husband. That's too much awkwardness for me." She sniffed. "Besides, he hasn't told Amy about us yet. I'm not going."

"Oh, but Fenway, this is your first—" Then silence.

Yes. It was her first Christmas since her mother died. In fact, it would be her first Christmas away from her mom, period. But with all the secrets floating around about her mother, she was pretty sure that the Chinese takeout a few blocks away from her apartment would be fine. Plus, there was always the holiday itself—as a coroner, she might have work to do, especially if others were taking the day off.

"I'm sorry," Charlotte murmured.

Fenway snapped back to the present. "Sorry about what?"

"I shouldn't have mentioned anything."

"About my mother? Don't worry about it."

"Well." Charlotte cleared her throat. "If I *don't* go to Laguna Beach, maybe we could meet at the hospital and have Christmas dinner after we see your father."

"Don't feel an obligation to—"

"Dammit, Fenway, I *want* to see your father, even if he's still non-responsive. Even if he never wakes up. I want to sit with him every day. And I don't want to drive three hours just so my mother can glare at me over the top of her glasses and accuse me of marrying for money."

Fenway was silent. Then she cleared her throat. "I'd love to have Christmas dinner with you, Charlotte." She wondered if she needed to bring anything. If it would be just the two of them, maybe she'd pick up some Chinese food on the way over.

"Thank you," Charlotte whispered, sounding like she was on the verge of tears. "I—I need to go."

———

Fenway's PC alerted her to an email; it was a message from Dez with the phone number of Victoria Versini's assistant—a 310 area code. Los Angeles.

The woman picked up on the second ring. "Happy holidays!" she said brightly. "Danica Punch speaking."

"Ms. Punch, this is Fenway Stevenson calling from the Dominguez County Coroner's Office. Do you have a moment?"

Punch paused. "The coroner's office? And where did you say you were?"

"Dominguez County. About two hours north of L.A., on the ocean."

"Oh—oh, right. Sorry, recent transplant. I don't know my California geography yet." Another pause. "Uh... my boss went up that way for the holidays. Is everything okay?"

"Have you been in Los Angeles for the last few days?"

Punch hesitated. "I—uh—I told my boss I would stay in Los Angeles."

"That doesn't answer my question—did you come up to Estancia?"

"Estancia? Where *she* is? No, of course not." Punch exhaled loudly. "You said you're from the coroner's office—is Dominguez County where Estancia is? Did something happen? Is Victoria in trouble?"

Fenway debated with herself and decided to tell her. "Victoria Versini was murdered early this morning."

Silence on the other end.

"Ms. Punch? Are you still there?"

Punch cleared her throat. "I'm sorry to hear that. Victoria was usually a good boss." She hesitated, then continued. "Uh, I've probably not been very kind lately when I was talking about her, which you'll find out if you talk to any of my friends. She wouldn't let me take any time off to see my parents for Christmas. She said the business was too important."

"I see."

"Early this morning, right?" Punch said quickly. "Two days ago, I went to see my parents in Kansas City. That's where I am now. I'm flying back to L.A. the day after Christmas."

"I thought you said Versini wouldn't let you go."

"She was never supposed to find out."

Fenway stood and began to pace around her office. "Do you know why she chose to go to Estancia?"

"Especially after I got her a prime spot on the Christmas Eve special on the Red & Rosé channel," Punch muttered.

"She canceled on a big opportunity and didn't give you a reason?"

"She said she had family business to attend to."

Something with the Ramparts, perhaps. But nothing Fenway had discussed with Tricia—or that McVie had spoken with Hank about—seemed time sensitive. Maybe she was just missing her adoptive family? Or were the Ramparts hiding something?

"Anyone at Red & Rosé who was angry at Victoria?"

"Not that I know of—she canceled a few weeks ago, so they had time to replace her. I'm worried she'll never get that chance again."

Punch paused. "Actually, I was worried that she'd blame me." She paused, then sucked in a breath.

"What is it?"

"I—I don't mean to sound self-centered or anything, but I just realized I'm out of a job. At Christmas."

"I'm sorry," Fenway said.

"Right, I know, I'm supposed to be sad. I am. It's just—we never really had a personal connection. Victoria was pretty demanding but didn't let anyone get close. Well, not me, anyway."

"Anyone you can think of who'd want to hurt her?"

"She wasn't outright mean, you know? I won't say that everyone loved her, but no one really hated her either. She was mildly annoying and sometimes a little selfish, but making me work through the holidays is really as bad as it got with her."

"Some of her food reviews are pretty mean."

"Oh—of course. Maybe you catch more flies with honey than with vinegar, but you certainly attract more Photoxio followers with negative content. A lot of businesses weren't pleased with the comments Victoria made about their vegetables. But I don't think anyone would..." Punch's voice trailed off.

"Ms. Punch?"

"Right, sorry. You might want to check out this vegetarian social media site—it's called BadSeed. A lot of Victoria's content gets reposted there, and that's where you might find some of the farmers defending themselves."

"Do you post Victoria's content there?"

"Not anymore, but sometimes it shows up. I used to send a lot of cease-and-desist letters, but now I realize it just drives more people to the Photoxio page. I don't read the comments, though. Way too nasty."

"I hear that." Fenway briefly thought of the comments she got on her campaign website.

"I know Victoria critiqued a couple of the farms up in

Dominguez County in the last couple of months. She gets online threats and laughs them off. Me, I'd never leave the house."

———

Fenway blinked, and her mouse hand twitched. While Dez had been scanning Victoria Versini's Photoxio feed, Fenway had checked Danica Punch's alibi and reviewed BadSeed. Dez thought the Photoxio comments were mind-numbingly dull, but in contrast, the BadSeed commentary was full of anger and sarcasm, users lobbing verbal grenades at each other, sometimes full of profanity and invective.

The latest video, posted the day before, discussed the produce quality of Diamond Hill Artichokes, a small family-run farm that was up Ocean Highway from Estancia, only about a twenty-minute drive from the cabin where Versini's body had been found.

Versini approached Diamond Hill like an investigative reporter. She was her usual bubbly self and seemed to delight in critiquing the flavor of the artichokes.

She kept scrolling down. Yep Younger—the owner of the farm—brought a subvariety of Salamanca artichokes from Peru, where at first it had struggled close to sea level, but after some cross-breeding and genetic tinkering, the artichoke had thrived. Versini used words like *cost-effective* and *budget-conscious* in her overview of Younger's development of the artichoke—and *gourmet pricing* and *poor value* when discussing the final product. But it was all without providing any hint of what flavors a gourmand might expect. The comments on the video had started to trickle in, but most were expressing shock at Versini's untimely death rather than commenting on Yep Younger's artichokes. Fenway was surprised that the news of her death had already made it to the public—then she remembered that Jack Dragon had discovered the body and didn't get so much as a warning from the sheriff to keep her death under wraps.

Like the Diamond Hill video, the rest of Versini's submissions from December were highly critical. Cheese from an artisan producer in Rome, Wisconsin was deemed overpowering and pungent. The producer had left a profanity-laced diatribe as a comment, saying Versini wouldn't know a gouda from a Camembert. Another negative video concerned a small family orchard in Washington State whose apples didn't meet Versini's standards. The Monday after Thanksgiving, however, was the release date for an Estancia-based co-op, Suncastle Dream Ranch. Their award-winning eggplants were heartily critiqued by Versini, who mimed vomiting not once, but twice during the video.

The Photoxio account for Suncastle Dream Ranch: "I've noticed that the only vegetables you enjoy are the ones with no flavor. You think arugula is spicy. Leave the food to the professionals, sweetie."

"Harsh words from the vegetable-growing community," Fenway mumbled to herself. She opened another browser window and typed in *Suncastle Dream Ranch*. A woman named Kendra Chanticleer ran the social media accounts, according to their *Meet the Team* page. Their address was off Highway 326, not too far from the entrance to Coast Harbor State Park. She looked at her watch— plenty of time to go interview the folks at Suncastle Dream Ranch and be back downtown in time for lengua tacos at Dos Milagros.

Oh, that's right—she had lost the bet. Maybe McVie would eat the tacos out of pity.

She sent the address to her phone and was picking up her purse when there was a knock on the door.

It opened a crack, and McVie stuck his head in. "Hey, Coroner."

"Hey, short-timer."

McVie raised his eyebrows. "I've got another week. Besides, crime never sleeps." He smiled. "I'm heading over to take a statement from Nancy Kissamee. Channel 12 isn't too far away from Dos Milagros if you want to grab lunch. And maybe grab that key."

Fenway scratched the back of her head. "I'd love to, but I'm heading out to Suncastle Dream Ranch. Seems someone there got a little defensive about one of Victoria Versini's negative reviews about their eggplants."

McVie furrowed his brow. "Is that some sort of euphemism?"

Fenway rolled her eyes. "Don't get all pervy on me, Craig. We're talking about real eggplants. The vegetable."

"I'm just saying—if you uncovered a negative review about the other kind of eggplant, that might be our prime suspect."

Fenway laughed. "You can join me if you want, and then we can interview Nancy Kissamee and grab lunch." She grinned. "Maybe even get the spicy eggplant at the new Indian place on Sixth."

McVie nodded. "We can discuss lunch places later. But yeah, let's go. You ready?"

"No spicy eggplant joke?" Fenway picked up her purse and followed McVie out the door.

———

Kendra Chanticleer pushed herself back from the computer desk, folded her arms, and glared at Fenway. "You honestly believe I'd kill someone over a bad review?"

"People have been killed for less." Fenway stood in front of Kendra's desk, McVie leaning against the wall a few feet behind her. Besides Kendra's tiny metal desk in the middle of the room, the small office held a five-foot-tall walnut-veneer bookcase with almanacs, gardening tomes, and binders shoved in all directions. The eggshell-painted walls were bare.

Kendra scoffed. "Have you even seen our Photoxio today?" She reached forward and turned the monitor so Fenway could see.

A mouthwatering photo of eggplant parmesan with a pink sauce drizzle, diced chives, and a dollop of—

"Is that garlic butter?"

A smile touched the corner of Kendra's mouth. "Honey and

roasted shallot butter. This is a recipe from Creole & Capulet, up near Monterey. Looks delicious, right?"

Fenway swallowed, her mouth watering. "What does this have to do—"

"'It's official,'" Kendra read from the post. "'If the Queen of Bland hates the bold, tantalizing flavor of our produce, you're sure to love it. Suncastle Dream eggplants are good enough for five-star restaurants. Tonight, they should be on your dinner table.'"

"Clever," McVie said. "I'm sure Versini loved being called the 'Queen of Bland.'"

Kendra arched an eyebrow. "I'm not the first one to call her that. You should see the comments on her blog."

McVie turned to Fenway.

"Dez is reviewing the comments," Fenway said quietly.

"The point is," Kendra continued, "our social media engagement is through the roof after that bad review. We have people defending us from Vicki, and they're voting in grocery stores with their wallets. We've sold out of eggplants within an hour at every farmers' market we've been at for the last three weeks. I ran into her at a restaurant a couple of days ago and bought her a drink—Vicki's negative review is the best advertising we've ever had."

"You bought her a drink?" McVie asked. "Were you just being clever, or do you know her?"

Kendra blinked. "Me and Vicki went to high school together. We graduated the same year."

"Oh—were you close?"

"At one point we were. But she wasn't a very good friend. Told lies about me to a boy I liked—not because she wanted him for herself or anything. It was just to be a dick. And then junior year, she stopped talking to me and became best friends with someone else."

Fenway racked her brain before the name came to her. "Avery Rampart?"

Kendra smiled wistfully. "Nice girl. I think Vicki only became friends with Avery because her dad had connections with a few producers and directors in L.A. It really sucks what happened to Avery."

"Didn't Victoria's father abandon the family when she was little?"

Kendra shrugged. "That's what she told everyone. Though it wouldn't surprise me if everything out of that girl's mouth was a lie." She chuckled. "When I was little, I *loved* spicy food. Still do. My grandmother caught me lying about something stupid—maybe if I'd done my homework or something—and she told me that lies killed off taste buds. So if I kept lying, I wouldn't be able to taste anything."

"And you believed her?"

"Back then? Sure. And even now—well, I'm not too sure that years of lying didn't kill off the Queen of Bland's taste buds, either." She tilted her head. "You know Victoria Versini isn't her real name, right?"

"It's not? It's on her driver's license."

"I'm not surprised—she insisted that everyone *call* her Versini. But she's Vicki Johnson. Too common of a name for her tastes, I guess."

"Do you know where the name 'Versini' came from?"

"No idea. Maybe it was her mother's maiden name."

"Can I ask," Fenway said as gently as she could, "what happened to Avery? Her mother said she passed away, but I didn't want to press too much."

"Oh—I kind of thought everyone knew." Kendra exhaled, long and slow. "But I guess that was almost ten years ago." Her eyes lost focus, and she stared past Fenway.

Fenway waited a beat.

"Sorry," Kendra said. "Got lost in thought for a minute. Anyway —suicide."

"I see." Fenway wasn't surprised, not the way Avery's parents had tiptoed around the subject of her death, but it still jarred her.

"You said it was almost ten years ago. Was Avery still in high school?"

"The summer after her senior year. She'd gotten good grades until her junior year, and then after she met Vicki, she kind of slacked off. Not a ton—just not straight A's anymore. Her parents wanted her to go to Stanford, but it was obvious she wouldn't get in. Then she said she didn't know what to do."

Fenway nodded. "Her parents couldn't have been too happy about that."

Kendra shrugged. "I only heard bits and pieces. But Avery got a couple of B's junior year, and things just didn't go right for her after that."

"She was depressed?"

"I guess. It was Vicki who found the body. The story I heard was that Vicki had gone down with Avery's parents to check out UCLA—that was Avery's backup, although even *that* was iffy. When they got back, she'd killed herself. Pills. No suicide note, but the coroner ruled it that way." She stared at Fenway. "You weren't coroner then, right?"

"No." Fenway pressed her lips together; she was the same age as Kendra, or just about, anyway. "It's a little weird that Vicki went down with Avery's mom and dad, isn't it?"

"Yeah," Kendra said. "A lot of people thought that was a little weird. But I guess with Vicki's dad gone and her mom as sick as she was, they thought they'd invite Vicki along on the trip."

"Victoria was close with the Ramparts, wasn't she?"

Kendra nodded. "Especially after Avery died—and Vicki's mom died right around that time, too. It was almost like Vicki just plopped right into the hole Avery left. I think they wound up paying for Vicki's tuition with Avery's college fund. And Mr. Rampart used to be a big-shot producer, you know. He made millions in action movies, and after he retired, he used his connections with the press to get Vicki's cooking blog featured on one of those morning shows in L.A."

Fenway paused. "Was the Ramparts' relationship with Victoria —uh—just..."

Kendra grimaced, but chuckled. "I don't know. I've heard the rumors about it being more than a platonic thing. But the rumors are all over the place. The first rumor I heard was that Avery's dad and Vicki were having an affair. Then I heard that Avery's mom and Vicki were doing it. Then it's all three of them, then the next rumor is that Avery's parents are taking Vicki to Tijuana to pimp her out every weekend. The stories just got weirder and weirder, and usually that means none of it's true."

"Did Vicki still get along with the Ramparts?"

Kendra frowned. "I literally haven't talked to Vicki in years— except when I bought her that drink. Most of what I've heard has been secondhand."

Fenway nodded and then decided to change tactics. "People get pretty wound up over Victoria's bad reviews, though, don't they?"

"I don't know why," Kendra said. "Sure, a lot of people follow her, but look at us—she gave us a bad review, and we're selling to all the people who despise her."

"When you say 'despise'..."

Shock registered on Kendra's face. "Oh—not enough to kill her. I think a lot of people enjoy hating her."

"But surely there were people who don't have your marketing savvy. Or your sense of humor." Fenway leaned forward. "Perhaps someone took her at her word."

Kendra thought for a moment, then recognition sparked in her eyes. "Oh—well, there is Yep Younger. He always takes things a little too seriously. Can't laugh at himself. A perfectionist. But a bad review from Vicki might set him off. He's kind of, uh, passionate about his product."

"He's got the artichoke farm, right?"

Kendra nodded.

"I saw that Victoria gave him a scathing review," Fenway said.

"In fact, it was on the day she died. You think her review would make him fly off the handle?"

"Yep's a weird one," Kendra replied. "I could see him obsessing about a bad review. He wouldn't use it in a marketing campaign like we do."

Fenway glanced at McVie, who stood with his brow furrowed.

"Can you think of anyone else who might want to harm Victoria?"

Kendra exhaled loudly. "She's—she's not a very nice person. I mean, if she wants something from you, then absolutely, she's sweet as can be. But lots of people have seen her nasty side. I don't know if they've ever seriously entertained murder, though."

"How about Jack Dragon?"

Kendra knitted her brow. "Who?"

"The news anchor from Channel 12."

"Oh. I don't know, I cut the cord last year. I stream everything. I don't think I've watched local news in years."

"He's the host of the Christmas parade in Estancia. Doesn't Suncastle Dream Ranch have a float every year?"

Kendra smiled. "Oh. Yes, we do. And I'm always forced to be on it, smiling and waving in an uncomfortable dress. That must be why I don't know this Jake Dragon guy—I'm stuck riding on a float for two hours instead of curled up on the sofa watching it Christmas morning."

Fenway looked at McVie. "Anything else?"

McVie shook his head. "Thank you for your time, Miss Chanti-cleer." He pushed off the wall as Fenway nodded to Kendra, and they left through the open office door.

CHAPTER FIVE

THE WOODEN SIGN WAS GRAY AND WEATHERED, AND THE PAINTED letters that spelled out *Diamond Hill Farms* had faded to a pinkish white. McVie drove his Highlander past the sign, down the gravel road leading to the small ramshackle house: a white one-story cottage with forest-green trim. Overgrown rosebushes grew in the front planter area. About a hundred yards behind the house was a bright red outbuilding, shorter than a typical barn. Two small tractors, both a shiny taxicab yellow, were parked next to the outbuilding.

"Guess we know where the money for this farm goes," Fenway said as McVie pulled the Highlander in front of the cottage and killed the engine. She opened the door.

"Good morning!" a voice called. Fenway looked around: a man of about fifty, wearing dirty denim overalls, a checked shirt, and an oversized straw hat, walked out of the outbuilding, crossing the distance to the Highlander. "Looking for the best artichokes in California?"

McVie raised his badge above his head. "Dominguez County Sheriff, sir," he said. "Official business."

The man stopped in his tracks, his brow furrowed.

"I didn't call the police," he finally said.

"I'm sure you didn't," McVie said. "I'm Sheriff Craig McVie, and this is the county coroner, Fenway Stevenson."

"Coroner?" The man's voice was hollow as his look of confusion deepened.

"We're looking for the owner of the artichoke farm," Fenway said.

"That's me. Yissichar Younger. Folks call me Yep."

"I'll get right to the point, Mr. Younger—Yep." McVie pulled out a small notebook from his pocket and opened it. "When did you last see Victoria Versini?"

"Versini—she's that food critic, right? I don't think I've ever met her in person."

"Really? She didn't care much for your artichokes."

"I sell my artichokes at farmers' markets and at several local produce stands in the area. Not to mention my distributor who covers Southern California." Yep smiled, showing a row of crooked but white front teeth. "How do you know she didn't like my artichokes?"

Fenway tilted her head. "Have you not seen her latest blog post or her last video on Photoxio?"

"I don't put too much stock in social media." Yep shrugged. "I have a business to run. And the holidays are always busy."

"She posted a negative review of your produce. I wouldn't think it'd be good for business."

Yep frowned. "Huh. It's hard for me to keep up with demand, and I haven't seen a drop-off in the last few days. Does she have a big following?"

McVie nodded. "You haven't read her review?"

"I just told you I haven't. I didn't even know she *did* a review of my artichokes."

"Someone from Diamond Hill Farms commented on a critique of hers."

"Really? On her site?" Younger rubbed his forehead. "I can't think of anyone—"

"Not on her site," Fenway said. "On BadSeed."

Yep brightened. "Oh, of course, BadSeed. Yes, things do get quite spirited on there. And those comments are seen by many of the restaurateurs in the state. Oh, yes. I may have even typed in a comment myself."

"You don't remember?"

Yep shrugged.

McVie scribbled in his pad. "Can you tell me where you were yesterday, say between six thirty in the evening and midnight?"

Yep set his mouth in a line. "I was in Paso Querido meeting with Walcek Produce. Daniel Walcek and I talked about supplying his company with artichokes for the coming year."

"Versini's review," Fenway said, "might jeopardize that deal."

"Dan wouldn't do that. We agreed on a price." Yep folded his arms. "In this business, your word is your bond. Word travels fast if anyone goes back on their promises. That would affect my business more than a ridiculous food reviewer's opinion."

"What time did you meet with him?"

"I was at his restaurant at four. We started negotiating and continued it over dinner." Yep smiled. "I ordered a dish that had artichokes in it, and I could tell they weren't mine." He chuckled. "I happened to have a jar of artichoke hearts with me. One taste and Daniel agreed to my price. We finished dinner at—I don't know, maybe ten o'clock. I drove back here, and I was in bed by eleven."

"Were you with anyone on your drive back? A co-worker, perhaps?"

"Twenty people can vouch for me at the restaurant," Yep said. "But no, no one was with me on the drive home."

"Can we get Daniel Walcek's contact information?"

Yep furrowed his brow again. "I suppose so—but exactly what is this for?"

Fenway shot a glance at McVie, who nodded. "Miss Versini was the victim of a crime," she said haltingly. "We're establishing the whereabouts of everyone who may have been with her in the last couple of days."

"Well, like I said, I never met her." Yep motioned with his head toward the outbuilding. "I have Daniel's phone number in my office. Come on and I'll get it for you."

Fenway's black flats crunched on the gravel as she followed Yep and McVie toward the outbuilding. While a large garage door was down, a metal door next to it, behind one of the tractors, was propped open.

As McVie entered the building, a glint of silver between the tractor and the building caught Fenway's eye. She stopped and looked—it was some sort of tool. She stepped closer and knelt down.

The tool resembled a pair of vice-grip pliers, but the handle and edges were fatter, and there was a cylinder below the handle that appeared to rotate. Instead of the flat surfaces of vice-grip pliers, a round metal piece resembling the blade of a can opener could be seen in the opening. A brownish, oily liquid covered the blade and some of the surfaces of the tool.

"Sheriff!"

McVie stuck his head back out of the doorway. "What is it?"

Fenway motioned with her head. "Take a look at this." She pulled out her phone and took several pictures of the tool on the ground and a few of the scene, getting the outer wall of the outbuilding and a section of the tractor, then took out an evidence bag.

McVie blinked. "That's a hose cutter." He set his jaw. "That's designed to do work on brake lines—even the ones coated in metal." He pointed to the circular blade. "Successful, from the look of it."

Yep came out with a folder in his hand. "I have Walcek's contact information, as well as my receipts from last night. The cost of doing business, as you might know—and dinner and drinks at his restaurant aren't cheap. I wanted to claim the expenses on my taxes."

McVie turned to Younger and pointed at the tool on the ground. "Would you mind explaining that?"

"What?" Yep stepped forward and peered over Fenway's crouched form. "What is that?"

"It's a hose cutter."

"A hose cutter?"

"You have tractors here, Mr. Younger. I assume your team does most of your own maintenance."

"Sure—but I've never seen that before. I don't think we have any tools like that."

"Do you do the maintenance work yourself?"

Yep nodded. "The simple stuff, sure. Anything too complicated and I either take the tractors into town or I get Mitch Jeffries to come out and take a look."

"Does Mr. Jeffries leave his tools here?"

"Uh—not unless he forgets. But he hasn't been to my farm in, oh, at least three or four months. I decided to invest in the new tractors over the summer, and I haven't had any trouble." Yep stared at the tool. "What's that brown stuff on the pliers? It's not rust, is it?"

"We'll have to take it to the lab and analyze it to be sure," McVie said, "but I'm betting it's brake fluid."

"Brake fluid? You mean—someone cut the brake lines on the tractors?"

Fenway startled. She hadn't thought of that—perhaps someone was trying to kill Yep along with Victoria. "Perhaps you'd better check your brake lines, Mr. Younger. I'd suggest checking your car along with your tractors."

With McVie in tow, Younger got a board, a flashlight, and a small toolbox so he could look underneath the tractors, then took everything to the front of the house to look under his car. He and McVie saw nothing, so Yep grudgingly started up the tractors and the car and pumped the brakes as McVie knelt and stared under the vehicles with his flashlight shining.

Fenway put on a pair of blue nitrile gloves. Watching Younger and McVie work on the vehicles, she turned over the discovery of the tool in her mind. Someone had cut Victoria Versini's brake lines and had left the tool in front of Younger's outbuilding. Yep certainly reacted like he didn't know what the tool was doing there. In fact, he was acting like he had no idea that Versini was even dead, never mind that her brakes had been tampered with. But Fenway had seen murderers be convincing before.

McVie walked toward Fenway, flashlight in hand.

She straightened up. "Thoughts, Sheriff?"

He stood next to Fenway and lowered his voice. "He's really giving me a hard sell that he hasn't seen that tool before." He frowned. "But if he does his own maintenance, I'd expect he'd have *some* idea what that tool is."

"I was thinking that, too." Fenway rubbed her chin. "But if he used it on Versini's car, why would it be out in the open?"

"He could have dropped it. Maybe Versini caught him cutting her brake lines so he had to improvise. Shooting someone in the face is a lot messier and more traumatic than snipping brake lines."

"True." Fenway kicked at the gravel thoughtfully. "So your theory is that he was traumatized by shooting Victoria in the face and was so out of sorts he dropped the hose cutter?"

McVie shrugged. "I'm saying it's a possibility."

"Motive?"

McVie scrunched up his face. "That I'm less sure about. He says Victoria isn't even on his radar." He rubbed his chin with the back of his hand. "But if he *did* have something to do with her death, wouldn't he deny it?"

"Especially if he killed her for writing a mean review." Fenway pursed her lips. "Did you tell Yep that Victoria was murdered?"

"No." McVie glanced over his shoulder; Yep walked around his car, staring at the wheels and the underside. "I wanted to tell him in front of you—you might get something out of his reaction that I don't see."

Fenway nodded.

McVie and Fenway waited as Yep got down on his hands and knees on the gravel, shined his flashlight below his car, then stood up, stretched, and walked back to the outbuilding. "I sure don't know what this tool is doing here," he said, scratching his scalp. "And I have no idea where that fluid came from. I sure *hope* it isn't brake fluid."

"Victoria Versini's brake lines were cut last night," McVie said.

Yep gaped. "Wait—you think *I* had something to do with it?" Then he blinked and took a step back. "Oh—wait—you're the *coroner*. Did she crash? Is she—is she okay?"

"I'm afraid Victoria's body was found this morning," McVie said carefully.

Fenway wasn't sure why McVie was implying that Victoria died in a car crash due to the cut brake lines, but she trusted him enough to play along. "I'm classifying the death as a homicide, Mr. Younger," she said, a stern note in her voice.

Yep gulped. "I swear I don't know how that cutting tool got here. And if that's brake fluid—well, whatever it is, I certainly didn't use that tool on her car."

McVie looked at Yep for a moment. The silence stretched out. Yep folded his arms, looking both determined and nervous.

"Mr. Younger," Fenway finally said, "are you quite sure you and Victoria Versini don't have any kind of relationship?"

"I told you, I've never met her."

"But she criticized you. People have threatened her in the past for bad reviews." Fenway took a step forward. "We have experts who can tell which computers have made certain comments, you know."

Yep shook his head vigorously. "I've never contacted Victoria Versini at all. Not once. I've never posted on her Photoxio or—well, certainly I *know* about her blog, but I've never made a comment on it."

"Is there someone out there who believes that you have a contentious relationship with her?"

"Me? A contentious—" Yep kicked at the gravel. "Listen, I grow artichokes. I *like* growing artichokes. People seem to enjoy them, and people seem to pay a lot more than they pay for other artichokes. I'm not rich, but I do all right for myself. When it comes to food bloggers or vegetable critics, I'll tell you what I think of them: nothing. Victoria Versini barely crossed my mind before today."

"You didn't answer the question. Is there anyone who thinks you and Victoria Versini didn't get along?"

"I can't imagine anyone thinking that. So—no. No one."

"I see." Fenway turned to McVie. "Craig?"

"We'll want to get that into the lab," McVie said gruffly, motioning to the tool in the evidence bag in Fenway's hand. "Whoever put the hose cutter here might have left some prints or some other sign to identify themselves." McVie glared at Younger. "If we find your fingerprints on this, Mr. Younger, I won't be inclined to cut you any slack. If you want to get out in front of this, now's the time."

"It's not mine."

"Whether it's yours or not, if you think we'll find your fingerprints on the tool," Fenway said to Yep, "you might pack up and head out."

"I've never touched that tool before," Yep declared. "You don't have anything to worry about."

McVie stared at Yep for a few moments, then slowly nodded. "All right. But stay in town. We will definitely have more questions for you."

———

As soon as the door shut in McVie's Highlander, Fenway took her phone out, looked through her recent call log, and rang Danica Punch again.

"Merry Christmas!" Punch bellowed when she picked up.

"Ms. Punch?"

"That's me!" She sounded giddy, perhaps even a bit tipsy. Background noise—a restaurant, or even a bar.

"It's Coroner Stevenson calling from Estancia again."

"And this is former gofer Danica Punch answering from the best barbecue place in Kansas City." She lowered her voice conspiratorially. "I'm staying for another two weeks. Got a date for New Year's Eve."

Fenway blinked—had she ever been with someone on New Year's Eve? She'd kissed people at midnight, but she wasn't sure it had ever been in the context of a relationship. Now she had McVie —and she didn't know what they were doing. Watching the ball drop in Times Square on TV, she supposed. With the way her cases had been going, she'd probably have to work that day anyway. And it would be McVie's last official day as sheriff, too—would he even feel like celebrating?

"...hope no one else has died," Punch said.

Fenway blinked and came back to herself. "No, nothing like that," she said quickly. "I wanted to know if Ms. Versini had ever mentioned a farmer by the name of Yep Younger."

"Yep?" Punch suppressed a burp. "What kind of name is that?"

"So that's a no?"

"I think I'd remember a crazy name like that," Punch said.

"Diamond Hill Farms, perhaps?"

"Oh—yeah, that one I remember. I was in the room before she filmed that one. She doesn't like artichokes. I've seen her go off on a tirade about them before." Punch chortled. "You'd think it was a personal grudge."

"Did she mention visiting Diamond Hill when she was here?"

Punch scoffed. "You assume she confided in me? That's nice. No, she didn't tell me what she had planned."

"All right, Ms. Punch. Thank you—"

"Hang on," Punch said. "I just remembered that I told her that turning down the Red & Rosé channel would cost her a lot of money. She said she had a good opportunity in Estancia. I just thought she wanted me to shut up, but maybe she had some sort of plan to get money while she was there."

Fenway pressed her lips together. "Did she say anything else?"

"I'm two whiskeys in," Punch said. "You're lucky I remembered *that*."

CHAPTER SIX

FENWAY NOTICED THE SPLOTCH OF SALSA ON HER BLOUSE AS SHE followed McVie up the front steps to Nancy Kissamee's house. Great—of all the interviews today, she had to look like a slob at the estate with the tennis court and vineyards visible from the top of the circular driveway.

A woman in a black Oxford shirt and trousers answered the door. McVie held his badge out. "Sheriff Craig McVie for Nancy Kissamee, please."

The woman took a step back and ushered them into a seating area that was entirely too pristine for Fenway's comfort—she felt like she'd get salsa on the carpet just by walking into the room.

"Ms. Kissamee will be with you shortly," the woman said, disappearing behind a white pocket door.

The house was deathly silent: no hum of a heater or a crackling fire, and the room was almost robotically pleasant. Fenway felt the urge to whisper.

After a few minutes—which seemed to stretch forever—a woman of about forty appeared in the doorway to the hall.

"My apologies," she said. Her makeup was thick but perfectly applied; her burgundy lips pulled forward the slightly olive hue in her complexion, and her straight brown hair with streaks of auburn brushed the tops of her shoulders in the style of a woman much younger. She wore a fitted red dress, scoop necked and knee length, a shiny white ruffle around the neck. Festive.

Fenway looked closer; the woman had a slightly strained, fake quality that Fenway had grown to associate with plastic surgery.

"Hortencia didn't offer you a drink?" she said.

"We're on duty, ma'am," McVie replied.

The woman visibly flinched at the word *ma'am*, her mouth contorted into a television-ready smile. "What can I help you with, Sheriff?" She stepped into the room and cast a suspicious gaze at Fenway. "And you are?"

"Coroner Fenway Stevenson." Fenway stepped forward and held her hand out for the woman to take.

Nancy Kissamee turned her head toward McVie as if she hadn't seen Fenway try to shake her hand. "Did she say she was the coroner?"

Fenway dropped her hand to her side. "That's correct."

"Oh dear," Kissamee said, still addressing McVie. "That must mean someone has passed away."

"Victoria Versini," Fenway said.

"Ah yes," Kissamee said, directing a sad smile at McVie. "I heard about poor Victoria this morning. Threw quite a monkey wrench into the production."

"We tried to find you at your trailer," McVie said. "You and Jack Dragon had both gone for the day."

"After the news about Victoria," Kissamee said, "the director and the writers had some work to do—Jack and I may be doing the show on our own, although there might be someone who can step in last minute. We expect to be called back this evening." She threw her head back, shaking her auburn tresses coquettishly, and smiled. "The life of an entertainer is often thrilling, but too often fraught with heartache and change."

"Too true," McVie mumbled. "How well did you know Victoria?"

"Not well," Kissamee replied, "but I've asked the staff to make some of her recipes. Quite talented, that one."

"Do you know anyone who would want to hurt her?" McVie asked.

Kissamee scoffed. "People who are famous attract unstable personalities frequently. If we're nice, we're either not nice enough or we're too nice. If we're pretty, we're either not pretty enough or we're too pretty." She shook her head. "Celebrity often comes at a terrible cost, Sheriff."

"Did you see anyone unusual around Victoria over the last few days? Did she say anything strange or out of the ordinary?"

"I don't know her well enough to know what is or isn't out of the ordinary with her," Kissamee said. "She was fairly talkative about her tragic past, however."

"Tragic past?"

Kissamee nodded. "She went on and on about looking for her birth father. Apparently, he'd run out on her and her mother and owed them hundreds of thousands of dollars in child support and alimony."

Fenway furrowed her brow. "That seems like quite a personal conversation."

Kissamee glanced at Fenway, then focused back on McVie. "I have one of those faces, darling. People trust me. They feel they can open up to me."

"What did Miss Versini say about her long-lost father?"

"If you can believe it," Kissamee said, "she talked about the judgment against him. Even though Versini came of age a decade ago, apparently a judge in the family law court issued a demand for child support payments—with interest."

"It's still in effect? The judgment doesn't expire?"

"Miss Versini wasn't terribly interesting," Kissamee said. "I didn't pay attention to most of the conversation, and besides, by then we'd gotten to the studio lot."

"Sorry," McVie said, "this conversation all took place in the car?"

"Of course. The car service picked all of us up the first week."

Fenway rubbed her chin. "Who else did Victoria tell about her long-lost father?"

"I assume anyone who would listen," Kissamee said.

"Did you hear her say anything to anyone else?"

"No," Kissamee admitted, "but I walked to Versini's trailer one morning and saw her hurriedly putting a letter or a card into an envelope, and she hid it in a box. It seemed suspicious to me."

"What kind of box?"

"A wooden jewelry box. Hideous. Reddish wood, quite out of fashion, and these absolutely gaudy gold handles on the front. About eight or nine inches wide, I would think."

Fenway shot a look at McVie, who didn't seem to pick up on it.

"Was it on top of her desk or hiding in a drawer?"

"She slammed it shut and put it in a drawer when I walked in," Kissamee said.

Fenway nodded. They needed to see the jewelry box—so Fenway was prepared to go to the studio lot and Versini's trailer.

"If that's all, Sheriff, I must attend to other matters." Kissamee rose to her feet.

"A few more questions, and then I'll get out of your hair. Have you ever been to the cabin where Victoria Versini stayed?"

Kissamee barked a laugh. "Don't be ridiculous. I don't *do* gravel driveways."

Fenway cocked her head. "How did you know it had a gravel driveway?"

Kissamee rolled her eyes. "Victoria went on and on about it. Apparently, she grew up poor—as if that were something to brag about—and she kept talking about the dirt road she lived on in Utah or Arizona or wherever she was from. I kept wishing Jack would change the subject or tell the girl to shut up." She scoffed.

"Fortunately, Jack noticed my annoyance. After rehearsal, he suggested we ride in separately—he even offered to pick up Victoria. Channel 12 didn't care for that; they wanted us to bond so we wouldn't look so fake on camera." Nancy Kissamee held up a finger in front of her face. "I'll tell you something, if I had spent any more time with that bitch, they'd have to give me some Xanax just so I could stand to be on screen with her."

"So Jack Dragon picked her up this morning instead?"

"For the last two days," Kissamee said, then she gave McVie a saccharine smile. "I wouldn't have thought someone so annoying would be his type, but he's not as young as he used to be. Or perhaps he just wanted an excuse to play with his new SUV."

"Mr. Dragon attracts a lot of personal attention?" Fenway asked.

Kissamee again directed her response to McVie. "He keeps things discreet," she said with a sniff, "but one can tell, you know."

"Did you see Jack Dragon and Victoria Versini in any kind of compromising position?"

Kissamee shrugged. "I don't want to be with anyone after rehearsal—I just want to go home. Yet Jack Dragon drives a young, up-and-coming talent home and picks her up at her cabin in the middle of nowhere." She winked at McVie. "Perhaps he never left her cabin."

McVie nodded, his face impassive. "And where were you last night?"

Nancy's eyebrows knotted together, but her forehead remained smooth. "Now listen, just because I felt no affection for the woman does not mean I had anything to do with her death."

"Of course not," McVie said reassuringly. "You understand, I have to ask."

Kissamee sighed dramatically. "I was here, of course. I got home from dinner around eight o'clock, then I did my nighttime routine and got my beauty sleep."

"And you stayed home all night?"

"Certainly. I didn't leave until about seven this morning."

"Can anyone confirm that?"

"Jamboree and Saffron."

"Who are they?"

"My pugs."

"No one else?"

"Hortencia had gone home by the time I came back from dinner." She shrugged. "But really, what would I have done? I heard she was killed at her cabin. If I'd killed her, I'd have waited until she'd gotten to civilization."

"What are they going to do with the Christmas parade now?" Fenway interjected.

Kissamee waved her hand dismissively at Fenway. "I heard they're trying to get a replacement, but I think they'll end up just going with Jack and me again. I suppose they won't get the Photoxio crowd, but I assume we'll have a few tributes to her, as well as some of her reviews that she was saving until air. It should be fine."

———

Fenway and McVie showed their badges to the security guard at the entrance to Channel 12's studio lot at the Las Derechas Christmas Tree Farm, about a half mile outside of Estancia's downtown and only a few blocks from Channel 12's headquarters.

Fenway got out of the Highlander, stretched her arms, and yawned. Three trailers stood off to the side of the paved parking lot. The atmosphere was noisy, and workers set up cables and decorations alongside the parade route—the road that led through downtown, past City Hall.

"Not a bad setup," Fenway said.

"It's not the Tournament of Roses, but we do okay," McVie replied. "Biggest thing Dominguez County has going outside of the county fair."

The trailer on the end had police tape encircling it, as well as a uniformed deputy standing in front of the door. Fenway and McVie walked toward the trailer.

The sound of a nail gun made Fenway turn: it was a man kneeling over pieces of wood, constructing part of a float. She looked up and saw a sign, its wooden face and its painted, embossed letters looking brand new.

This year's Christmas Parade made possible
by a generous grant from
Ferris Energy

McVie followed Fenway's eyes, then glanced at her face. "You okay?"

Fenway turned to McVie and nodded. "Yeah. Sure."

They took a few more steps, and McVie cleared his throat. "I heard he's out of the woods."

"Out of intensive care," Fenway said. "He still hasn't woken up. The doctors say—" Her throat caught. "Anyway, let's search the trailer. We might find something."

Deputy Celeste Salvador stood to one side of the trailer entrance and lifted the police tape. "I'd like to request that my official duty be somewhere away from Jack Dragon," she murmured to McVie as he passed.

"When did he leave?" McVie asked.

"Only about an hour ago. They finished with rehearsal before lunch, but he was trying to convince me to leave my station and go to lunch with him. I had to threaten him with arrest for interfering with a police investigation before he backed off."

McVie set his jaw as he pulled his latex gloves on. "I'm sorry you had to go through that, Celeste. I'll get another deputy out here tomorrow."

Celeste turned to Fenway and shook her head. "Why do they always make some dumb joke about getting handcuffed? As if I haven't heard it a hundred times before."

"Maybe you should take them up on it." Fenway snapped on a pair of blue nitrile gloves. "A couple of hours in county lockup with his hands cuffed behind his back, I bet he'll think twice before hitting on a deputy on duty."

"Not only do they always joke about handcuffs," Salvador replied, "but they're rich enough to afford expensive lawyers too."

"Still, it's nice to think about every once in a while. The looks on their faces."

"Can't argue with that."

Fenway followed McVie inside the trailer.

It was small, about eight feet long by six feet wide. A small desk with four drawers built into the wall stood on one side, and a table with a bench on either side was toward the back. On the other side of the desk, a makeup table stood beneath a lighted mirror, apparently intended to be used with the same chair as the desk.

Fenway glanced over the desk. No box.

The first drawer she opened? Bingo.

A large jewelry box was pushed to the back of the drawer, and Fenway pulled it out. Wood with a reddish stain on it, but it was pockmarked and scratched. The fittings, metal that might have been gold or brass plated, were likewise scratched.

"This box has seen better days." Fenway pulled it out of the drawer and set it on the desk.

"Well loved, it looks like."

"Yeah, okay, Mr. Glass Half Full." Fenway found a latch, and the top of the box released.

Inside sat a folded sheet of paper. She opened it up and read.

$L - 32230$
$P - 85077$
$StL - 77104$
$K - 15248$
$D - 93415$

McVie stepped behind Fenway and perused the list over her shoulder. "What in the world are those?"

Fenway cocked her head. "Zip codes, maybe?"

McVie pointed to the last number. "That's one of the zip codes for Estancia. The rich part of town—not the mansions-overlooking-the-oceans rich, but those gated communities a few miles south of downtown." He paused. "But what does the D mean?"

Fenway shook her head. "No idea." She pointed to *StL*. "Think that's the zip code for St. Louis, Missouri? What do you bet?"

"You're betting that it *is* the zip code for St. Louis?"

"Right."

"I already won our last bet," McVie said, a touch of smugness in his voice. "You're getting the key to my apartment."

"Best two out of three."

McVie looked sideways at Fenway.

"Fine." Fenway took out her phone, the photo of the zip codes appearing onscreen. She pointed at the second number. "I think that's in the Mountain Time Zone."

"How do you know that?"

"The national zip code system," Fenway said. "New England gets the zip codes that start with zero, and generally speaking, the numbers go up as you head south and west from New England. The west coast gets all the nines, and the mountain states—Colorado, Utah, Nevada, Idaho—get the eights."

"Now I'm glad I didn't take you up on your bet." McVie paused. "Does P stand for Provo?"

"In Utah? Maybe." Fenway tapped the paper again. "This K number—one five. I think that's New York or Pennsylvania." She looked at McVie. "Why would Victoria have a list of zip codes? And what do these letters mean?"

"I don't know," McVie said. "What about that first number?"

Fenway furrowed her brow. "I'm guessing the southeast. Georgia, maybe." She pulled her phone out. "Hang on a second."

The phone rang, caught halfway through the second ring. "Good evening, Coroner Stevenson."

"Good evening, Ms. Punch. I hope I'm not disturbing you?" There was no background noise, and Punch sounded thoroughly sober.

"It's fine." She sighed. "I'd be much more helpful when I'm back in L.A. with all my files."

When you're not with your family, Fenway thought. She cleared her throat. "We came across a paper with some letters and numbers. Do these mean anything to you?" She read the letters and numbers off into the phone.

"I'm sorry, Coroner. Nothing. Maybe this is something I'd locate in my files."

"Would you mind letting me know when you'll be back in L.A. with your files?"

"It won't be till after New Year's. Now that I'm unemployed, I changed my flight to spend more time with my parents. Did I tell you I have a date for New Year's for the first time in four years?"

"That's great, Ms. Punch. Let me know if you get a brainstorm on those numbers."

"Sure."

They said their goodbyes and ended the call, then Fenway turned back to the desk.

"Is there anything else in that jewelry box?" McVie asked.

"Let's see." In one of the small drawers, Fenway found a simple gold chain with a tarnished locket on it. She opened it and saw two pictures: one of a smiling girl, about five years old, and the other a woman of twenty-five or thirty who had the same nose and cheekbone structure as Victoria.

"What do you think?" Fenway said. "This must be Victoria and her mom, right?"

"Probably. I would imagine the Ramparts could tell us."

They examined the rest of the trailer, and Fenway went back to the Highlander to get her fingerprint kit. After an hour of tedious dusting on the surfaces, knobs, and handles, Fenway had about two hundred full or partial prints, but only about thirty unique ones. Fenway had to turn the lights on in the trailer about halfway through, as the sun was close to setting.

They drove back toward City Hall in silence, Fenway yawning.

"Hey, none of that," McVie said.

"We need to start fresh tomorrow. We've both been working close to twelve hours." Fenway cleared her throat. "And—and I need to go see my dad."

McVie nodded. "Want me to go with you?"

Fenway shook her head. "Family members only right now. I'll stay with him while Charlotte gets dinner. Maybe we can see each other after."

"Sure. I'd like that."

The paper and the initials stuck in her head. Since McVie recognized the Estancia zip code, she was sure the other numbers were zip codes, too. But what did they mean?

"Let's get those prints couriered over to the lab in San Miguelito," McVie said. "Then we can head home. Your car is at my place, right?"

Fenway nodded. "But maybe I won't drive home for a while." She leaned her head back and closed her eyes. Then she opened them again and took her phone out.

Tapping on the screen, she chuckled.

"What is it?"

"As much as I sounded like I knew what I was talking about with those zip codes, I was totally wrong about St. Louis. That zip code is for Houston, Texas." She cocked her head to the side. "I wonder..."

"What?"

"Didn't Tricia Rampart say that Victoria's father abandoned the family for a woman in Texas?"

"I think you were talking to Tricia in the kitchen. I was with Hank in the living room."

"Right—I'll have to double-check my notes." She tapped her chin. "But we've definitely got a zip code for Houston. Do you think that Victoria was tracking down her father?"

———

The quiet hum of the equipment next to Nathaniel Ferris's hospital bed was enough to cover the sounds of Fenway's footfalls as she stepped into the hospital room. She rapped lightly on the door.

Charlotte sat on a chair at a ninety-degree angle to the bed and stared out the window, her blue eyes unfocused. The night was dark, so Charlotte's reflection stared back at her. Her blonde hair was swept back into a ponytail, its casualness a clash with the tailored charcoal business suit she wore.

Charlotte's head jerked around to the door. "Oh—Fenway," she said. "I'm glad you've come."

"You had to go to the office today?"

"I don't know how your father ran that business without firing half the people who report to him," she said.

"I'm sorry I'm late. There was a murder this morning."

Charlotte nodded. "Right, right." She sighed. "I still haven't figured out what I'm going to do about going to Laguna Beach."

Fenway shrugged. "You don't want to go. So don't go. You have a ready-made excuse here."

"I just don't—well, I hate admitting this, but I don't want to spend Christmas alone."

"You don't have anyone—your shooting club, or maybe someone from the tennis club—who would invite you to Christmas dinner?"

Charlotte looked at her husband—Fenway's father—lying in bed and reached out to hold his hand. "I guess they would. I haven't been shooting since—well, since this happened. Or played tennis." She looked up at Fenway. "You know, when Jane's husband was diagnosed with ALS, a bunch of us sent her cards, and we made sure she had food, but no one reached out to her. It's like we'd all forgotten what to say." She turned to her reflection in the window again. "And now it's my turn. None of my friends are calling, either. And the people who were Nate's friends have stopped asking about him."

Fenway walked slowly over to Charlotte, then tentatively put a hand on her shoulder. "That happened to me after my mother's diagnosis, too. I know I'm busy with work, but I'm here now."

Charlotte reached up and patted Fenway's hand. "I know you're here as much as you can be. It's not like we can do anything for him."

"I finished reading the oil industry book to Dad out loud," Fenway said. "I tried putting on an old Red Sox World Series game, but the internet was so slow, I had to stop. Baseball drags enough without the first pitch taking thirty seconds to buffer."

Charlotte chuckled. "Especially when Nate can't even—" Then her voice hitched, and she looked down at the floor.

"You can go get dinner," Fenway said.

"I've already eaten," Charlotte said. "I thought I'd stay for another hour or so."

It was odd, feeling sorry for Charlotte. "So—uh, if you're not going to Laguna Beach, and if I'm not invited to Craig's ex-wife's new house for Christmas, I guess I'll accept your invitation that you and I keep each other company."

"I really would enjoy that." Charlotte lifted her head. "Sandrita has the week off, which is just as well—no one is at home to cook for, anyway." She set her mouth in a line. "I thought I'd pick up a turkey breast, maybe some gravy and mashed potatoes, sauté some green beans. Nothing fancy, nothing big. No sense in making a big meal when it's just the two of us." She smiled. "Maybe I'll watch the Estancia Christmas Parade on TV. Your father and I used to love to go down and watch, but—obviously we can't do it this year."

"I'll tell you what," Fenway said. "I hadn't heard about the Christmas parade before, but if I don't have to work, maybe you and I can go down there. Ferris Energy is a big sponsor—surely you have access to some box seats or something, right?"

Charlotte smiled, then her chin trembled. She stood and smoothed her business suit with her hands. "Just need to take a little trip to the restroom. I'll be back soon, then you can head home."

She rushed out of the door before Fenway could say anything.

PART 2

TWO DAYS BEFORE CHRISTMAS

CHAPTER SEVEN

FENWAY SAT ON THE SIDE OF THE BED, A TOOTHBRUSH STICKING out of her mouth, her cell phone in her hand. "Ahh!"

McVie pulled his undershirt on and glanced over. "What is it?"

"Fiffvurr."

"What?"

Fenway stood, walked into the bathroom, and spat the mouthful of toothpaste out. "Pittsburgh."

"What about it?"

"One of the zip codes from yesterday—it's for the Squirrel Hill neighborhood of Pittsburgh."

"And—what does that have to do with anything?"

Fenway tapped on her screen and scanned an email. "I had Dez trace the people we talked with yesterday."

"Kendra Chanticleer?"

"She's lived in Estancia all her life. Went to college, then came right back here. But Yep Younger, too. He's *from* Pennsylvania."

McVie grinned. "He wouldn't happen to be from Pittsburgh, would he?"

"Yes. Born in Erie, went to school in Pittsburgh. He trained as a mechanic, too, so he'd know his way around brake lines."

"What was the letter in front of the Pittsburgh zip code?"

"K."

"Do you have anything connecting him with a 'K' in Pittsburgh?"

Fenway tapped and scrolled through the email. "Let's see." She paused. "Well, the street he lived on was Woodbridge. That's of no help. Let's see—his first job was at Northumberland Garage. No 'K' there either." She scrolled again. "Oh—his family belonged to the Kehillat Anshe Maarav Synagogue in Squirrel Hill. Maybe that's what the letter refers to—Kehillat."

McVie grunted as he looked at himself in Fenway's full-length mirror.

Fenway tapped a few more times on her phone. "I wonder..."

"What?"

"The Diamond Hill Artichokes website says that Yep Younger transplanted his artichokes from Peru to Estancia."

"Okay."

"That must mean he spent at least a little bit of time there, right?"

"In Peru? Probably not an unreasonable assumption." McVie put on his beige sheriff's shirt and buttoned up the front. "But those are U.S. zip codes."

"Not necessarily." Fenway clicked. "Wow—Peru has five numerals in their postal codes, too." She tapped again, then shook her head. "I don't know about this. Peruvian postal codes mostly start with zero, and I don't see any zeroes on this list."

"How are you connecting the dots? Did you memorize the list?"

"I took a photo of it, remember?" Fenway tapped her phone again. "So, we've got a possible match with Yep Younger and this Pittsburgh zip code, and the 'D' on this list, next to the Estancia zip code—that could easily stand for Diamond Hill Artichokes, right?"

"It could. But didn't Victoria write 'StL'? Why write those three letters and then just a 'D' when 'DH' would be better?"

Fenway nodded. "Maybe she was lazy when she wrote the 'D' but not lazy when she wrote the 'StL'?"

McVie knelt down and pulled on his work boots. "Let's see what the lab says about those hose cutters we found in front of Younger's outbuilding. That might give us more to go on." He shook his head. "Killing someone over a bad review, though—I know I've seen people killed for less, but he just doesn't strike me as that kind of person."

Fenway stared at the floor for a moment.

"I know that look," McVie said.

"Maybe it's not a bad review," Fenway murmured.

"What makes you say that?"

"Victoria Versini got a court judgment against her father in Arizona—a big, life-changing amount of money. What if she found out that Yep Younger is her father?"

McVie cocked his head. "That's a big 'if.'"

Fenway nodded. "I know. But I suspect the zip codes are related to Versini's search for her father."

"It could be a million other things—"

"It could," Fenway said, "but she was hiding that paper. It was written in—well, maybe not in code, but in a shorthand she could understand. I don't have any other reasonable explanation for it. Especially since she showed up here for a small-town Christmas parade instead of taking a big career-advancing step."

McVie was quiet. "There's no proof, but I can't think of another explanation either."

"So what if Versini tracks Younger from Pittsburgh all around the country and finds that he ended up with a successful artichoke farm in her old home town? She shows him the judgment against him. A million dollars would be a serious blow. It could impact his livelihood."

"That's a more reasonable motive than a bad review." McVie

finished tying his boots and stood. "It sounds like Victoria talked about a lot of personal things with Nancy Kissamee."

Fenway was quiet for a moment.

McVie glanced at her face, started to say something, then caught himself.

"What is it?"

"It's—" McVie rubbed his forehead. "I noticed that Nancy Kissamee treated you like you didn't exist. I should have said something yesterday, but I didn't know what. I didn't—I didn't want to make things worse."

Fenway shrugged. "Not the first time it's happened, and it won't be the last. Don't worry about it."

"Should I have said something? Part of me felt like I should say something, but then—I didn't want to put you in an awkward spot. Or a more awkward spot."

Fenway didn't reply.

"At first, I thought that maybe she was ignoring you because she was flirting with me. That happens to me sometimes."

Fenway looked up at McVie and set her mouth in a line.

"But that's not what happened there," McVie said quickly. "I noticed it. I'm sure you noticed it."

"Sounds to me like the only person who wasn't uncomfortable in the conversation was her," Fenway said.

McVie nodded. "I didn't know what to do. I'm sorry."

"I don't know what you should have done either," Fenway said. "They didn't teach—" She almost said something about white guilt, but she stopped. Was she trying to ease McVie's discomfort? Or maybe she just couldn't figure out a comment that was biting enough.

"Anyway," Fenway said, "you can interview her on your own next time."

"Yeah," McVie said. She could hear the note of misery in his voice, and for a moment, she felt a ping of self-righteousness. But it quickly faded, and coming up right behind it, washing over her, was a wave of fatigue.

McVie cleared his throat. "The reason I brought it up was because I thought maybe she'd talked more about her personal life to Jack Dragon. We should go talk to him."

Fenway rolled her eyes. Out of the racist frying pan and into the sexist fire, as it were.

———

They pulled up to the lot at the Las Derechas Christmas Tree Farm, and the security guard waved them through. McVie parked his Highlander next to Jack Dragon's gold Lexus.

Fenway got out of McVie's SUV and walked around the Lexus. It was pristine except for splashes of mud on the underside of the fenders behind the wheels.

"I don't understand it," Fenway said. "He obviously loves this car, and yet he was okay with driving it on that gravel road. On my car, I'd just consider it normal wear and tear, but the way the rest of the car positively gleams, I would think he'd have a heart attack over the mud." Fenway crouched and looked more closely. "Oh, it's not just mud. There are a few scratches—must have been from the rocks he kicked up."

McVie shrugged. "From what I understand—and it's more than Nancy Kissamee's insinuations—Jack Dragon is known to pursue younger women. It would be in character for him to continue to drive Victoria Versini to and from her cabin just to have a chance to get close to her. Maybe that's worth a couple of scratches on his Lexus."

Fenway suppressed the shudder threatening to go up her spine. "I suppose." She stood. "Okay. Let's go."

They walked toward the trailers. The trailer wrapped in police tape was guarded by a white male deputy, standing next to the sign reading *Victoria Versini*. Fenway squinted; it was Deputy Donald

Huke. She waved to him and started to open her mouth to ask how Melissa was, but then remembered how seriously Huke took his job. He nodded slightly at her wave.

The second trailer had a sign the same size as Victoria Versini's, but instead of a name, there was a reproduction of a crude pre-Renaissance-style painting, showing a nun dressed in a white head covering and robes of royal blue and deep red. A sword in her left hand, she stood in front of a large green lizard with bright red scales, its jaws wide in a roar, exposing its forked tongue.

It reminded Fenway of the library book she'd checked out several times as a kid—seeing the art style pinged a distant memory she couldn't quite grasp. She still didn't remember the name of the book, but she was sure it was stored in some filing cabinet in her brain. *The Magnificent Lives of Legendary Animals.* That wasn't right, but it was closer. She cleared her throat. "Is that supposed to be a dragon?"

"I guess. Doesn't look like any dragon I've ever seen."

"If you're seeing dragons, maybe it's time to get you into therapy."

McVie rolled his eyes, stepped up to the door of the trailer, and knocked.

"It's open," Jack Dragon called from inside.

McVie opened the door, and he and Fenway stepped inside. The trailer smelled like vinyl and fresh whiskey, not unpleasant. Jack Dragon sat in front of his lighted mirror, looking closely at his face. A dark-skinned woman of about twenty-five patted his face with a wedge-shaped makeup sponge.

"Ah, the sheriff and the coroner," Dragon said, closing his eyes. "More questions about poor Victoria, I take it?"

"Nice nameplate on your trailer," Fenway ventured. "Is that supposed to be a dragon?"

"One of the very first art pieces depicting a dragon in Europe," Dragon said. "And it's not just any dragon—it's a *tarasque*." His eyes opened, and he leaned forward. "A fearsome creature.

According to Gervais de Tilbury, the tarasque is a cross between the Leviathan of the Bible and the celebrated if mythical bonacho."

"The mythical what?" Fenway said, and immediately regretted it.

"Bonacho. Every twelve-year-old boy should be fascinated with this creature." Dragon's voice began to drip with a storyteller's dramatics. "The bonacho had these great horns that curved inward, which it obviously couldn't use to defend itself."

The woman applying makeup grunted and frowned but continued working.

"So," Dragon continued, "it would shit out flaming, caustic feces that it could aim at its pursuers."

"Lovely," Fenway said, suppressing a grin.

"The tarasque had the same talent—depending on the story, of course." Dragon chortled. "That painting is of St. Martha taming the tarasque—just a few sprinkles of holy water, and it was like a puppy dog."

"I hope it was housebroken," Fenway said.

Dragon blinked, then laughed uproariously. The woman pulled her hand back.

"That's quite good, Coroner," Dragon said, pointing a finger in the mirror at her and winking. "I'll have to steal that."

"You're welcome to it," Fenway said.

"Now," Dragon said, "how can I help you?"

"Nancy Kissamee told us that you gave Victoria Versini a ride to and from her house over the last couple of days."

"I'm afraid Nancy was a bit bored by any story that didn't revolve around herself or her pugs," Dragon said.

"Versini talked a lot about her missing father, from what I understand," McVie said. "Did she continue to talk about her father with you after Nancy stopped joining you?"

"Certainly," Dragon said. "You know, I felt bad for the kid. Her social media feed might not have floated my boat, but she had a hard childhood. Apparently, her mother died when she was in high school."

"We think she might have come to Estancia partially to find her missing father," Fenway said. "Did she ever talk about that when it was just the two of you?"

Dragon dropped his eyes to the floor. "I'm sorry to say she never mentioned a name to me."

The woman went back to blotting his face with the makeup sponge.

Dragon's face was impassive. "She did, however, mention to me that she reviewed her father's produce on her food blog. She said she was expecting to get at least some sort of comment. She said she was thinking of going to see him. I figured her plans were for after Christmas, but I suppose she might have taken an afternoon to visit—although I don't know if he lived in the area, or even in the state."

"Any idea what kind of produce?" Fenway asked.

"I'm sorry, I don't recall. Maybe asparagus? Are there asparagus growers in the area?"

"Artichokes?" Fenway suggested.

"It's possible," Dragon said. "I don't really remember."

"What else about him?"

"I got the impression he wasn't very old when Victoria was born. That makes sense, I guess. When you're too young to have a kid, you make some bad decisions."

"What gave you the impression that he wasn't very old?"

"She said things about him not being as old as—well, I guess I don't know what she was comparing him to."

"I don't think I understand," McVie said. "She said he wasn't as old as something?"

"But I don't know what," Dragon said, an edge of annoyance creeping into his voice. "She didn't make a whole lot of sense."

"Younger," Fenway said.

McVie cocked his head. "What?"

"She said he was Younger," Fenway said. "Not younger than a baby or younger than a house or something. Younger—his name."

McVie turned his head back to Jack Dragon. "Is that what she said? That he was 'Younger'?"

"Oh—I suppose that could be it. Why?"

"Do you know who Yep Younger is?"

Jack Dragon squinted, and the woman prepping his makeup sighed. "I don't—hang on. Marcy, can you give us a minute?"

Marcy put down the makeup sponge and walked toward the door. Dragon followed Marcy with his eyes until she was out of the trailer, then gave McVie a conspiratorial raise of his eyebrows. Fenway set her mouth in a line but didn't say anything.

McVie frowned. "Mr. Dragon, do you know who Yep Younger is?"

"The name seems to ring a bell—you would think with a name like Yep Younger, I'd remember." Dragon tapped his fingers on the arm of his chair. "Channel 12 may have done a human-interest story on him. Artichokes, you said?"

"I did mention artichokes earlier," Fenway offered.

"Oh, yes," Dragon said, recognition dawning in his eyes. "I did a story—a couple of years ago now, on an artichoke farm not too far outside of town. The gentleman who owned the farm—Ruby Ridge, I think it was?"

Fenway gritted her teeth. *Diamond Hill.*

"Now that I think about it, I believe his name was Younger. Don't quote me on that, though."

McVie had a few more questions, but Dragon had lost interest in providing useful information. They left the trailer, Fenway's eyes raking over the tarasque drawing again.

"I didn't know you were into dragons and fantasy stuff," said McVie as they walked to the parking lot.

"Not since I was a kid, and I was more into unicorns back then. But you've got to admit, the story about the bonacho was highly entertaining."

"Butt-related humor never goes out of style."

Fenway tapped her chin. "It makes you think. All over the world, cultures had depictions of different types of dragons. Must be something in our genes that makes us all dream about huge flying lizards."

"Speak for yourself. I was into race cars when I was a kid."

"I could see that." Fenway grinned. "Little Craig pushing toy cars all over the kitchen floor."

"I was great at the engine noises."

Fenway glanced over her shoulder at the trailer. "It's like he's not even affected by finding Victoria's body. He cares more about giving us a good story than whether we find her killer."

"Typical show-biz narcissist." McVie unlocked the SUV with his key fob, and he and Fenway both got into the Highlander. He put the key into the ignition but didn't turn it, instead staring through the windshield.

"What is it?"

"We had enough to arrest Yep Younger yesterday," McVie said. "But we didn't."

"Yeah, but we'd have let him go if there were no fingerprints on the hose cutter. And the D.A. wouldn't have supported it."

"Yesterday, we thought Younger might have killed Versini over a bad review." McVie started the engine. "Now we have evidence suggesting he was her long-lost father who owed her a million dollars."

Fenway shifted uncomfortably. "I know I'm the one who suggested it, Craig, but it's still speculation."

"With what Dragon said? About her identifying Younger?"

"Jack Dragon probably just wanted to get in her pants. I'm surprised he could recall that much of their conversation."

"Still," McVie mused, "maybe we could do a DNA test. If it's conclusive, that would underscore a motive."

"We don't need a DNA test," Fenway said. "It only matters if Younger *believed* that Victoria Versini was his daughter."

"And, of course, that he knew she was going to make him pay for back child support." McVie put the Highlander into reverse and backed out of the parking space.

Fenway nodded. "We need to get the paperwork from the court in Arizona. *Somebody's* name will be on there—and if it's Yep Younger, I'll feel more comfortable arresting him."

McVie turned out of the Christmas tree farm parking lot. "This close to Christmas, I don't know that we can expect a fast turn-around time."

"You don't have to rely on your interpersonal skills when you ask for stuff like this." Fenway took her phone out of her purse. "It's all online now."

"I know *that*, Fenway. Usually, we need to search by case number." He looked at her out of the corner of his eye. "Do you know it?"

"Of course not."

"Well, little Miss I-can-get-everything-on-the-Internet," McVie said, giving Fenway a coy smile, "we *can't* get the case number without talking to an actual person. And actual people—ones who aren't trying to avoid spending Christmas with their ex-wives—are taking time off. Some of the civil courts are closed for the whole week between Christmas and New Year's Day." He sighed. "It's not ideal, but maybe we should arrest him now."

"Two days before Christmas?"

McVie shrugged. "If he thinks we're onto him, you don't think he'd take advantage of the holidays to move out of the area?"

"He has a business here. If he's worried about his livelihood—which we think is his reason for killing Versini—he probably wouldn't just leave."

"He brought artichokes here from Peru. He could be on his way back there right now. He might be able to continue his business there."

"I suppose." Fenway tapped her phone and scrolled for a

moment. "How about that. There's a nonstop from LAX to Lima. Only fifteen hundred dollars."

"What's the extradition treaty with Peru?"

Fenway set her mouth in a line. "Doesn't matter if Younger goes somewhere he can't be found. The artichoke-growing regions there are rural. He changes his name, he could disappear."

"Still think we shouldn't arrest him two days before Christmas?" McVie glanced at Fenway.

"There needs to be something else, doesn't there, Craig? I mean —yes, he's got the hose cutters, but even if he *is* the one who cut Versini's brake lines, that isn't how she died."

McVie nodded. "You're right. We need more evidence—even if it's circumstantial, it could be the difference in getting a warrant signed. Let's see if he has a shotgun registered to him. With a farm out in the country? I bet he does."

Fenway called Dez and put the phone on speaker as it rang.

"Hey, Fenway," Dez answered. "How'd your interview with Jack Dragon go?"

"Interesting. He thinks that Victoria might have mentioned Yep Younger."

"As someone who might have wanted to hurt her?"

"More than that." Fenway paused. "You got my message about the judgment against her birth father for back child support, right?"

"I saw it in my inbox this morning." Dez clicked her tongue. "Ah —your theory is that Yep Younger is her long-lost father and didn't want to pay back child support."

"McVie says we need a case number."

"They just updated the search functionality of some of the state databases. I'll see if Arizona was one of them. Hold on for a second." Fenway could barely hear the sound of Dez's keyboard clicking over the Highlander's engine. "Okay—it's going to require a county-by-county search, but it can be done without a case number. I'll look up where Victoria spent her formative years and see if there's a last name that matches."

"Thanks. Oh—and you're on speaker. Craig is here, too."

"Morning, Sheriff."

"Morning, Dez—and, before we get too far afield, we need to see if Yep Younger has any shotguns registered. Or, I suppose, any guns that could potentially be on his property."

"I'll get on it," Dez said. "One other thing came in this morning. Victoria Versini isn't her birth name. She changed it when she moved to Estancia with her mother. Officially applied for the name change on her eighteenth birthday."

"I have her name in my notes—I found that out yesterday when I interviewed the eggplant farm employee. Vicki Johnson—that's the name she went by. Not a great name for a woman who wanted to start a famous food blog, I guess."

"Johnson was her mother's name—Rose Ellen Johnson."

"Have you dug up her birth certificate? Does it say who the father is?"

"Yes—it's listed as John Peluda." Dez spelled the last name out. "I haven't been able to get a record on him."

"Were they married? John Peluda and Rose Ellen?"

"I haven't found a marriage certificate. But with the last name of *Johnson*—well, it's going to be hard to dig through all the results. It might take a few days. And I'm *not* working Christmas."

"See what else you can find on Yep Younger."

"I already got his history in Pittsburgh—his work history, his parents. I even sent you the name of his preschool. What are you looking for?"

"A connection to Houston and Arizona, too. Oh—and some-place in the southeast." Fenway pulled up the photo of the paper with the zip codes. "You saw the photo I sent you, right?"

"The photo?"

"The ones with all the numbers that might be zip codes."

"Oh, yes. And the letters in front of them. I searched for those zip codes. The one labeled with a P—that's Phoenix, Arizona. That makes sense. But the L is listed with a zip code for Jacksonville,

Florida. The 'StL'—which I would assume refers to St. Louis—is a zip code for Altadena, Texas—a suburb just outside of Houston. And the K—well, you mentioned Pittsburgh already."

Fenway ran a hand through her curly hair and exhaled. "This doesn't make any sense. And none of these are postal codes for Peru."

"Could refer to something else."

"But," Fenway said, "the 'D' matches with the Estancia zip code."

"Hang on," McVie said. "You said the 'D' could stand for Diamond Hill. And you'd said that the 'K' might stand for the name of that synagogue in Pittsburgh. That's one work-related zip code and one personal connection. Maybe Victoria tried to find him through any means she could. Bars he frequented, clients he got, stuff like that?"

"If Victoria wanted to get child support," Dez said, "she might have done some research into her father's other jobs. Maybe that's part of how the judge determined how much he owed."

"We *heard* that the father had to pay," McVie corrected. "We haven't actually seen the judgment."

"If there's no judgment," Dez said, "then this path of inquiry won't help us."

"The only scenario that makes sense to me," Fenway said, "is that Victoria Versini was killed because someone didn't want to pay the judgment for that back child support. Whether that was Yep Younger or someone else."

McVie tapped his hands on the steering wheel. "Or someone didn't *want* Younger to pay. Is he married?"

"Divorced," Dez said.

"So maybe it wasn't Yep—maybe it was his ex-wife or one of his children. If Yep has to pay hundreds of thousands of dollars in back child support, that cuts the kids out of their inheritance, or it could significantly reduce alimony payments."

Again, Dez's keyboard clicked. "Okay—Younger is divorced, and she's remarried, so alimony isn't in play. One child, a daughter. Aged twenty-six. Currently a librarian at Paso Querido Public Library."

Fenway tapped her phone a few times. "They're open," Fenway said. "Closed tomorrow for Christmas Eve, so I guess we better go today." She glanced up—the exit for downtown flew by.

"Paso Querido, here we come," McVie said.

CHAPTER EIGHT

THE YOUNG WOMAN KNELT ON THE CARPETED FLOOR BETWEEN two large rows of steel bookshelves, the first marked '300' and the second '400.' The gray plastic cart behind her was half-full of hardbacks, and she tried to squeeze a large bound tome, a plastic cover over its yellow dust jacket, between two equally hefty books on the bottom shelf.

Fenway took a step forward into the aisle between the shelves, holding her badge out. "Ms. Younger?"

The woman flinched, dropped the book, and stared at Fenway. "Oh—uh, yes. I'm Naomi Younger. Can I help you?" She brushed off her hands, picked up the hefty hardcover, and stood. She glanced behind Fenway at McVie, who nodded and took a step back.

Fenway appraised the woman. Naomi Younger was roughly five foot two, dressed in a scoop-neck red sweater with a white button-up blouse underneath, the collar of the blouse over the sweater. Fitted black trousers and black canvas sneakers completed the Christmassy look. Her eyes were large and brown, her skin a light olive tone like her father's. She wore no makeup.

"I'm County Coroner Fenway Stevenson, and this is Sheriff Craig McVie. Mind if we ask you a few questions?"

Naomi lifted a finger to her lips and motioned them to follow her. They walked through the aisles into a conference room, and Naomi shut the door behind them, setting down the hardback and taking a seat at the end of the table. Fenway and McVie sat across from each other.

"Two nights ago," Fenway said, opening her notebook. "The twenty-first, going into the morning of the twenty-second. Can you tell me where you were?"

"Where I was? Whatever for?"

"Just need to establish a timeline."

Naomi crinkled her nose, but then sighed and nodded. "I finished work at five thirty. Drove to the Las Derechas Christmas Tree Farm in Estancia with Mary and Tobias."

"Sorry—Mary and Tobias?"

"Co-workers. We're working on a float for the library. I worked until about ten o'clock, then we all drove back to P.Q. Tobias drove us back to the library parking lot, and I got my car and drove to my apartment."

"Where is that?"

"Nocturne Street, by the Marks-the-Spot."

"That's in P.Q.?"

Naomi nodded. "I'd guess I was asleep by eleven thirty."

"Can anyone confirm you went home after getting dropped off at the library?"

"Well..." Naomi squinted. "What is this about?"

"We had an incident two days ago," Fenway said. "I'm sorry about the questions, but we're trying to rule people out."

"Rule people out of what?" Naomi suddenly gave a jerk of her head. "Hold on. That Photoxio chef who was murdered yesterday?"

"That's correct."

"I've never met the woman before in my life," Naomi said. "I knew she was co-hosting the TV coverage of the Christmas parade, but that's it."

"Do you follow her on Photoxio?"

"No."

Fenway glanced up at McVie, who inclined his head slightly: *Keep going.* She turned back to Naomi. "Your father has the artichoke farm in Estancia, correct?"

"Diamond Hill, yes."

"Have you spoken to him about what he's going to do with the farm after he retires?"

Naomi tilted her head. "What does this have to do with—" Then she sighed. "No. I don't expect my father to retire—he'll probably die during the harvest season at ninety-five years old."

"Any plans for you to take over the business?"

Naomi chuckled. "Not on your life. That business killed my parents' marriage, and even when he has it running smoothly, he's two bad harvests away from bankruptcy. No, thanks."

Fenway nodded. Yep Younger's daughter was saying everything she should say if she wanted to deflect attention away from herself. Perhaps Fenway should poke Naomi with a stick and see the reaction.

"Are you aware of any judgments your father has against him for unpaid child support?"

Naomi blinked. "What? Unpaid child support?"

"That's correct."

She shook her head. "If he got anyone pregnant after the divorce, it's news to me."

"No," Fenway said, "this would have been a few years before you were born."

Naomi furrowed her brow. "Back in Pennsylvania?"

"Did he ever visit Arizona?"

"Not that I know of." Naomi shook her head. "But he's always kept himself to himself. I suppose I don't really know what he did before I was born."

"One more thing, and I apologize, but I have to ask this of everyone we interview. Do you own a shotgun, or do you have access to one?"

Naomi chuckled. "I work in a library. What would I be doing with a shotgun?"

"I'm sure I don't know," Fenway said, smiling in the easy, friendly way she'd seen McVie do in the past. "But I still need an answer to the question."

"No, I don't own a shotgun."

"Access to any guns?"

She shook her head. "My father keeps his guns locked up."

"Your father owns a shotgun?"

"To keep coyotes and mountain lions away." A note of defensiveness in Naomi's voice. "He's out in the country enough that he needs it."

Fenway nodded. "Thank you, Ms. Younger." She looked at McVie, who stood.

"I appreciate the time." McVie held his hand out, and Naomi shook it, a little awkwardly.

"Oh—the time!" Naomi said, startled, then looked at her watch. "I have to start Children's Hour in five minutes. Excuse me." She hurried out of the conference room.

"What do you think?" McVie said in a low voice.

"I see no reason to suspect that she isn't telling the truth. She might know who Versini is, but it doesn't seem like there was any recognition in her eyes or her mannerisms about possibly being Versini's half-sister."

"Doesn't seem like the type who feels entitled to an inheritance, either."

"Right."

"But her father is a different story. He didn't tell us he owned a shotgun."

"That's true." Fenway stood. "Oh—she left her book here."

Fenway picked up the heavy tome, turned it over, and nearly dropped it in surprise.

The Curious Lives of Legendary Creatures.

"What is it?" McVie asked.

"I loved this book when I was a kid." She showed McVie the title. "I checked this out four or five times one summer."

"Legendary creatures, huh? I wonder if it has information about that tesseract Jack Dragon told us about."

Fenway opened the book and flipped through a few pages. "Tarasque."

"What?"

"Tarasque, not tesseract," Fenway muttered. The book was even more beautiful than she remembered, full of detailed pen-and-ink drawings, full histories of the creatures' appearances in folklore. She grinned as she closed the book. "Guess I've found something to put on your bedside table when I'm bored. I bet Medusa is in here. Maybe I'll learn how to turn my hair into snakes."

"Very funny."

"I'm deadly serious," Fenway said.

"About turning your hair into snakes?"

"About checking out this book. I haven't seen it since I was ten years old."

"You'll have to drive all the way back here to return it."

"Paso Querido is lovely—I don't mind having an excuse to come back. There's a great Thai place down the street I've been meaning to try anyway."

"Come on—you barely leave the house if you're not working on a case."

"That's not true. I go to Dos Milagros."

"But it's not in P.Q."

"Fine," Fenway said, putting *The Curious Lives of Legendary Creatures* back on the table. "You're no fun."

"Your wallet will thank me for not having to pay all those library fines."

Dez was waiting at the entrance to Diamond Hill Artichokes in her cruiser. As McVie drove the Highlander in, the police cruiser followed. They drove up to the shed, parking next to the pickup truck.

McVie killed the engine and turned to Fenway. "You want to stay in the car?"

"No. I need to see how Younger reacts to being arrested. Even though he's got a shotgun, our evidence is still thin."

Dez rapped on the driver's-side window. McVie turned the key and rolled the window down.

"How do you want to play this?" Dez asked.

"Fenway was just saying the evidence was thin."

Dez nodded. "An unlicensed shotgun isn't a crime in the state of California until you carry the gun in public."

"And we're on private property." McVie rubbed his chin. "Are you checking with Pennsylvania?"

"Who knows how old the shotgun is? If he inherited it from his parents—"

"We can still push for him to register the gun. And produce it."

"But," Fenway said, "there's no way to tell if the gun was used to kill Victoria Versini."

"Not with rifling on the ammunition, no," Dez said, "but whoever killed Victoria was close enough for blowback onto the gun itself. There will be traces of blood and, uh, other detritus."

"It might also," said McVie, "make Younger nervous enough that he'll agree to come in for questioning. If he thinks we don't have enough evidence to arrest him, he can appear to be cooperative."

Fenway ran her hands through her hair. "And then if he gives us any information that doesn't match the evidence—"

"We'll know we're on the right track, anyway," said Dez. "You ready?"

Fenway got out of the car. The pungent aroma of fertilizer hit her nose. She hadn't even noticed it the day before. The sun came out from behind the clouds and shone harshly on her, making her sneeze.

Dez shot a glance at her. "You okay, rookie?"

"I'm fine," Fenway said.

"Stay behind us," Dez said.

Everything seemed louder than normal: her shoes crunching on the gravel, the whirring of equipment behind the outbuilding. Her feet felt stuck in mud as she followed Dez across the gravel lot and up the three steps to the ramshackle house serving as a business office.

McVie opened the door and went inside, Dez and Fenway following.

Fenway's eyes had to adjust to the dim light of the interior. A man in a tan jacket and blue jeans held two large plastic bags full of artichokes. He stepped back, his eyes wide, as McVie and Dez entered.

A desk stood under a window on the left side, the sunlight casting harsh shadows around the room. A woman behind the desk got to her feet. "I'm sorry—do you have an appointment?"

"County Sheriff," McVie said. "We need to speak with Yep Younger."

"Mr. Younger is out checking the fields," the woman said. She had a wide face and wore a red-and-green sweater with crude Santa faces sewn into the design. "He'll be back in an hour or two."

"Are there any guns on the property?" McVie asked.

"I believe you need a warrant," the woman said.

"We have reasonable suspicion that a shotgun belonging to Mr. Younger was used in the commission of a crime," McVie said. "Further, that shotgun isn't registered in the state of California."

"That's not against the law," the woman said. "I know our rights. As long as we keep it on our property, it's perfectly legal."

"Sir," Dez said, addressing the man in the tan jacket, "are you an employee here?"

"Just came in to buy artichokes," he said, fumbling slightly with his words.

McVie turned to the woman. "If you conduct business here, California firearms law considers this a publicly-accessible area. I suggest you call Mr. Younger and tell him the sheriff requests his presence at the office."

"I'll just buy these later," the man said, putting the bags down on the woman's desk and scurrying out of the room.

"We're open Christmas Eve! Tomorrow at ten!" the woman called after him.

The door closed behind the customer, and the woman glared at McVie. "You just lost us a customer."

"We plan to stay here until Mr. Younger returns."

The woman gritted her teeth.

"If you call Mr. Younger on the radio, however," Dez said, "we can wait outside for him. In an inconspicuous place."

The woman looked down at her hands, then picked up the yellow-and-black radio on her desk. "Yep? It's Marla. I've got a few representatives from law enforcement here. They say it's important."

Yep's voice, faint, underneath loud crackling noises. "I can be there in about an hour."

"They plan to wait for you. And they're scaring off our customers."

A pause. "Fine. I'll be right there. Ten minutes."

"Thank you," Fenway said.

The woman glared at her.

The three of them left the office and walked back to their cars.

"What do you think?" Fenway said quietly.

"The woman behind the desk is Marla Quiñones," McVie said. "She's made a run for city council a couple of times. Falls short in votes, but she knows her rights. Interprets them in a very libertarian way, doesn't ever want to pay for public services. But when the Dos Secos Wildfire threatened her house two years ago, she called the fire department a hundred times. Still showed up at a city council meeting and said she didn't want to pay for the fire station on her side of town to stay open."

"She seems like a big fan of the police, too," Fenway said.

"Rumor has it that she's involved with an anti-government militia group over in San Miguelito County," McVie said. "I don't know if that's true, but I'd rather not rile her up too much."

The hum of the equipment behind the outbuilding changed to something slightly lower pitched—and much quieter.

Yep Younger walked out from behind the outbuilding, a straw hat perched on his head, his jeans and flannel shirt covered in dirt. "Yes sir, Sheriff," he said, an edge to his voice. "I assume you've delayed me for a good reason."

"Your shotgun, Mr. Younger." McVie folded his arms. "Where is it?"

"I've cooperated fully."

"I'm not saying you haven't. We certainly appreciate the cooperation we've had up till now. But we're looking for the murder weapon."

Younger narrowed his eyes. "I thought you said she died in a car accident. The hose clipper you took this morning wasn't enough?"

"I didn't say how she died," McVie said. "You didn't tell us you had a shotgun, Mr. Younger."

Younger sighed. "I keep the shotgun in a safe. We get catamounts and coyotes out here, and when we're protecting the artichokes against frost, sometimes they come down from the hills."

"I understand," McVie said, "but the fact remains, it's unregistered."

"It was my father's."

"Please, Mr. Younger, just get the shotgun for us."

Younger's shoulders sank.

Walking into the outbuilding, Younger led McVie, Dez, and Fenway down a hallway to a back room.

"I respectfully object to this," Younger said. "I have the right to bear arms, and I'm breaking no laws by having this gun on private property."

"Just because it's private property doesn't mean it's not a public area," McVie said. "You've got customers in your office, purchasing your products."

"Not out here," Yep said. "Customers don't come back here. This is for employees only."

McVie held up one hand. "That sounds like a job for our lawyers to figure out," he said. "Your shotgun, please, Mr. Younger."

Younger clenched and unclenched his fists, glaring at McVie. After a moment, he turned and moved a wheeled aluminum rack away from a wall, revealing a black metal gun safe roughly four and a half feet tall and less than two feet wide. He turned the combination lock three times, then unhooked the latch. The safe door swung open.

It was empty.

CHAPTER NINE

YEP YOUNGER SAT ALONE IN THE INTERROGATION ROOM AT THE Dominguez County Sheriff's Office. His hands were folded in front of him, and he tapped his foot, his movement making his chair squeak. Fenway leaned against the back wall in the observation room, separated from Younger by a one-way mirror.

Dez opened the door to the observation room. The red and green lights strung up in the hallway cast strange shadows into the room. Dez handed a folder to Fenway.

"Anything?" Fenway asked.

Dez shook her head as she closed the door. "The hose cutters were wiped clean. No fingerprints at all."

"Did he agree to the cheek swab?"

"He said, 'Let me think about it.'"

Dez folded her arms and turned to look at Younger. "I suppose it's better than him asking for his lawyer."

"DNA results take a couple of weeks anyway. And with the holidays, we'll be lucky to get results by February."

"Still, we'd know in February if Younger is Versini's father." Dez scratched her nose. "Still haven't arrested him yet?"

"We're waiting to see what the search warrant at his house turns up. Did the judge sign off?"

"Yes. We've got deputies executing the search now."

Fenway took a step off the wall, closer to the mirror. "I'm surprised he came with us voluntarily."

"Where's McVie?"

"He had to talk to ADA Pondicherry about the evidence in the big burglary case. He said he'd be back."

"Does he want to do the questioning?"

"I think so." Fenway glanced over at Dez. "His last big hurrah and all that. This could be the last time he gets to interrogate a murder suspect."

"Aww, his last interrogation. Is that part of your Christmas present to him?"

Fenway grimaced. "He and I have only been dating for a couple of months."

"Officially," Dez said, a smile touching the corner of her mouth.

"Yeah, well, I didn't know what to get him. But he's always saying Megan doesn't want to come over because he doesn't have the top-of-the-line video game system that Amy does. So I got the latest and greatest for him."

Dez raised her eyebrows. "You don't like it when Megan comes over, do you?" she asked.

Fenway shrugged. "She's his daughter. Having her play video games is better than Craig begging her to spend time with him, right?"

"I suppose." Dez tilted her head. "Do you know what he got you?"

"No, and I don't want to know." But a picture of a small gift box flew through Fenway's mind. The ribbon fell away, the lid opened, and McVie's apartment key sat on a tiny bed of satin inside. Fenway shook her head to rid herself of the image. "So how long before the deputies are done with the search?"

"At least a couple of hours," Dez said. She turned to look at

Younger. "I don't get it. He led us right to that gun safe. If he knew it was empty, why would he do that? Did he think it would make him look less guilty?"

"He said he and Marla were the only ones who knew the combination, and Marla swears up and down that she hasn't touched the safe." Fenway sighed. "It's not official from the lab, of course, but the fingerprints I took off the safe all seem to match his."

"And he gave us his fingerprints willingly. Why didn't he agree to the cheek swab?"

Fenway smiled. "McVie told him that if his shotgun *had* been stolen, we'd need his fingerprints to isolate the fingerprints of the thief."

Dez nodded. "Did McVie say anything about holding Mr. Younger on a gun charge?"

"Can't charge him with possessing an unregistered shotgun that doesn't exist yet," Fenway said. "Besides, that definition of 'public space' is tenuous at best. McVie wants to use it to hold him if we're sure he's the murderer."

Dez nodded to the folder. "Open that folder."

"Good news?" She opened the folder and flipped past the fingerprint report on the hose cutters.

Superior Court of Arizona • Maricopa County

Case Number 18-27563P
Petitioner / Party A: Victoria Versini aka Victoria Johnson
Respondent / Party B: John Peluda
Child Support Order A.R.S. §25-503-3
In Case Number 92-3838A, Respondent was previously
    ordered to pay child support in the amount of $850 per
    month to Rose Ellen Johnson pursuant to the Arizona
    Child Support Guidelines without deviation until Peti-
    tioner's 18th birthday. Support arrears were provided

from the birth month of the child (the current Petitioner
in this case) and the month of the finding of the original
case.

Support arrears:

The court finds that Respondent has not paid any of monies
owed to Rose Ellen Johnson, or, after Rose Ellen Johnson's death, the guardian of Petitioner. Total of all
monies owed by Respondent is $183,600.00.

Respondent is ordered to immediately pay all owed monies
to Petitioner. Interest applies; total of child support in
arrears currently owed is $437,761.30. In addition, the
court finds this refusal to pay child support to be egre-
gious, and Petitioner has provided evidence of loss,
including court and legal fees to transfer guardianship,
lawyers' costs, and fees and penalties incurred by Rose
Ellen Johnson for nonpayment of bills before Petitioner's
18th birthday. The court agrees with Petitioner that
Respondent is responsible for these additional costs of
$235,476.81. With interest, total monies owed by Respon-
dent is $979.211.32.

Fenway's eyes widened. "That's almost a million dollars."

"A million dollars doesn't buy as much as it used to," Dez said,
"but Victoria would have been set for a few years, anyway. And
interest and penalties continue every month this isn't paid."

"We need to figure out if John Peluda and Yep Younger are the
same person. Was Peluda present at the most recent civil
proceeding?"

"I don't believe so, but I'd have to do more digging."

"Have you checked into Yep Younger's financials?"

Dez shook her head. "For anything like that, we'd need Piper to
work her forensic accounting magic."

"Still," Fenway mused, "I'd think this kind of thing might put
Diamond Hill Artichokes out of business."

"The land is worth millions," Dez said, "so Younger might be able to mortgage it and survive. But I don't know if the land is under his name or if it's owned by the company. Either way, I don't believe he's in a position to just hand over a million dollars."

Fenway took out her phone and tapped on the screen, then showed it to Dez. "Nonpayment of child support in Arizona is a felony. Eighteen months in prison. And if the judge in this case was willing to apply lawyers' fees to the total that John Peluda owed, I wonder how a judge in a criminal court would act."

Dez stared through the one-way mirror at Yep Younger. "Do you see any resemblance? To Versini, I mean."

Fenway shrugged. "She was shot in the face with a shotgun at close range. So I've only seen pictures. Both Younger and Versini are white, and they both have brown eyes and brown hair. It looks possible to me, but I don't think Versini is a mini-Yep or anything. At least not from the pictures."

The door opened, and McVie popped his head in. "Sorry. We've got a problem with the chain of evidence on those burglary cases, and I have to deal with it before the end of the day. Can you two take care of the interview?"

"Are you sure?" Fenway asked. "I know you wanted to—"

McVie waved his hand at her dismissively. "Don't worry about it. I've got to interview another burglary suspect, so that's almost as exciting."

"Sorry."

McVie gave Fenway a wan smile and closed the door.

Fenway turned toward the one-way mirror. Yep Younger was still calm, sitting patiently.

"Do you have a plan?"

"Focus on the past," Fenway said. "We've got a name—John Peluda—that Yep Younger may not realize we have."

"If you accuse him of being John Peluda," Dez said, "he'll lawyer up faster than Santa can disappear down a chimney. You'll force your hand—it'll be arresting him on that gun charge if you want him to stick around." She rubbed the back of her neck. "And as soon as you bring up that name, he'll know you're close to making the connection. If the name 'John Peluda' comes out of your mouth, you better be ready with a backup plan."

"Same thing if we mention Arizona or Houston or Jacksonville," Fenway said. "Yep Younger is our prime suspect, and we need to treat him like it." She tapped her chin. "We need background on Mr. Younger. Aliases, his trips to Peru, the financial state of his business—whatever we can dig up. Let me know if we need to apply for any warrants." Fenway paced in a small circle around the observation room, shook out her hands as she exhaled, and then looked up at Dez. "Ready?"

Dez opened the door, and they both went into the interrogation room.

Yep looked up as Fenway and Dez walked in. They sat opposite Yep, their backs to the one-way mirror.

"Sorry for the wait," Dez said. "Right before Christmas, we have to deal with all kinds of things."

"Busy time of year for me, too," Younger said. "I've been racking my brain, trying to figure out where that shotgun could be."

"Do you think you forgot to put it back the last time you used it?"

Yep sighed. "That's just it—I don't remember the last time I used it. I think it was last spring. A catamount had come onto the property during the harvest, but one blast from the shotgun scared it off." He shook his head. "It might have been a year before that, now that I think about it."

"Can you remind me what kind of shotgun it was?" Dez asked.

"Yes, it was a Blue Heron twelve gauge. Nothing fancy, probably manufactured in the late 1940s. Walnut stock."

"No burglaries or break-ins in the last two years?"

"Not that I know of."

"And you haven't used it for at least eight or nine months?"

"I haven't even seen it during that time. I assumed it was in the safe."

"Surely you clean the shotgun regularly, Mr. Younger."

"When he owned it, my father kept the shotgun in excellent condition. He'd clean it thoroughly every three hundred rounds. My problem is that I haven't shot more than twenty rounds in the last five years. I should give it a good cleaning anyway—considering how long it's been—but it's not like I'm going out hunting. I only keep my shotgun here to protect my farm." Younger unclasped his hands and placed them on the table, palms down. "I always store my shotgun in that safe. It was a while ago. At least nine months since I last used it."

Fenway tapped her fingers on the table. She would have to be careful with the way she phrased this. "Can you tell me the places you've lived?"

Younger blinked. "Where I've lived? I've been in Estancia the last fifteen years, ever since my father passed."

"Before that?"

"How far back do you want me to go?"

"Where were you born?"

"Seriously?" Younger looked from Fenway to Dez and back again. "You want me to go through my whole life story?"

Fenway nodded.

"Uh—fine. I was born in Erie, Pennsylvania. My family moved to Pittsburgh when I was little—two or three."

"Squirrel Hill?" Fenway asked.

Younger frowned. "Yes—but what does my religion have to do with anything?"

Fenway's heart raced. That wasn't the reaction she was hoping for. "I apologize. Go on."

"I didn't get very good grades in high school," Yep said, "so my father sent me to work one summer at my uncle's grape orchard in Bakersfield. He thought the back-breaking work would force me to get serious about my studies." Yep smiled. "Instead, it made me realize how much I love being outside. Getting to see the literal fruits of your labor."

"When was this?"

"Maybe thirty years ago. My uncle saw how good I was at harvest time—planning, paying attention to the crops. He offered me a permanent job after high school."

"So you've been in California ever since?"

"Yes, ma'am—almost thirty years."

"You didn't work anywhere else—not over the summers in high school, or go visit a relative in another state?"

"I went up to Castroville about five years later. Took a tour of the artichoke farms up there. Tried to plant some in Bakersfield, but the summers are too hot. They need the coast." He got a faraway look in his eyes. "Beautiful plants. The flowers are just gorgeous. It's too bad they only live a few years."

"When did you go into business for yourself?"

"My father passed away about fifteen years ago. I took my portion of the inheritance and bought some land outside Estancia. Only a few acres at first—took on a *lot* of debt. And I took a trip to Peru because I thought the Salamanca artichoke would do well in this climate—and I figured out a way to make them more tender and a little sweeter." He tapped his temple. "Conform to the American palate, you know."

"How long did you spend in Peru?"

"About six weeks. Harvest time—and I brought a bunch of plants back with me." He rolled his eyes. "The paperwork you have to go through to bring Salamanca artichokes into California—all the testing, all the red tape—it was crazy. And I had to tinker with the plants once I brought them here. There were a couple of times I thought about giving up. But after a couple of years, I did it." A note of pride took root in his voice.

"Your artichoke farm is important to you."

"Of course. It's my life's work. I cross-bred the Salamanca artichokes with the green globes that are so common in Castroville."

He leaned back in the chair. "You know, in the late spring, you can walk into the fields and literally see the artichokes get bigger. That's how fast they grow."

"And you've been successful."

"Have you tried any of my artichokes? The hearts, maybe? They sell them at farmers' markets and at the specialty grocers here."

"I'm sorry, I don't think I have." Fenway cleared her throat, quickly glancing at Dez, whose face was impassive. "Let's get back to high school for a minute. You said you left Pittsburgh. Was that right after graduation?"

Yep shrugged. "Three or four weeks. My mom didn't want me to go."

"Did you work any after-school jobs in Pittsburgh?"

"I worked as a stocker at Squirrel Hill Market after school my senior year."

That wasn't it—nothing that began with K. "Did you go to synagogue in Pittsburgh?"

Yep shifted in his seat. "My parents went to Chabad Shalom Temple. I went until I was about fifteen. My parents were disappointed I didn't want a bar mitzvah. If I'm honest, I was shocked to find out that my dad hadn't written me out of the will."

Fenway tapped her fingers on the table again. It was time to open the box. "Have you ever spent time in Arizona? About thirty years ago? Maybe stopped there for a few weeks when you traveled to Bakersfield?"

Yep shook his head. "I always say I'll see the Grand Canyon, but the business takes up too much of my time." His eyes softened and lost focus. "Deborah and Naomi went without me. Said it was beautiful. I'd had a couple of people quit right after the harvest. There was too much to do. I couldn't go."

"Deborah—is that your ex-wife?"

"Yes. She lives in San Diego. Naomi is a librarian over in P.Q."

Fenway briefly thought of *The Curious Lives of Legendary Crea-*

tures, still sitting on the shelf in the Paso Querido Public Library. "So, that's a no? You've never spent any time in Arizona?"

"I've changed planes in Phoenix. That's about it."

"Anywhere else? Houston, maybe? Jacksonville?"

"My mom took me to Philadelphia when I was little. And I've been to the Rock and Roll Hall of Fame in Cleveland. Oh—and I've been to a couple of the Small Farm Conferences over the years. Once when it was in Fresno and once in Santa Barbara." He tilted his head. "Why so interested in where I've been?"

Fenway took a deep breath and sat up straighter in her seat. "Does the name *John Peluda* mean anything to you?"

Yep Younger frowned. "That name doesn't ring a bell, but I've had so many employees over the years, I might have forgotten. I can check my records when I'm back in the office."

Fenway glanced at Dez, and she motioned with her head. Fenway closed her notebook and stood. "Excuse us for a moment, Mr. Younger."

"I've been as accommodating as I can," Yep said, tapping his foot. "I know you're trying to do your job, but I have work to get back to."

"We appreciate your cooperation," Fenway said, then followed Dez out the door of the interrogation room, closing it behind her.

"So he admits to being in Pittsburgh," Fenway said. "But not Phoenix or any of the other cities. The synagogue he mentioned isn't even the one I thought it was—it doesn't begin with a K."

"Maybe," Dez said, "those are notes from a private investigator of the places he tried to find Mr. Peluda."

"We could be way off base, too," Fenway said. "It's possible that Versini searching for her father had nothing to do with her death."

"What about the Ramparts?" Dez asked.

"They seemed pretty broken up about her death."

"What if," Dez mused, "it was an accidental shooting? Let's say Hank Rampart—who *does* have a shotgun registered to him, by the way—was lending the gun to Victoria and it accidentally went off?"

"And he tried to cover it up?" Fenway ran her hand through her hair. "I suppose it's possible. His wife was devastated—first her daughter takes her own life, then if Hank accidentally shoots Victoria? He wouldn't want her to know." Fenway pursed her lips. "But that's purely hypothetical. We have nothing even approaching evidence for that."

"Maybe we should ask to look at Hank's shotgun. We didn't do it the first time, did we?"

"McVie talked to Hank Rampart, not me. I talked to Tricia."

"Did you mention the shotgun to Tricia?"

"No—she seemed so overwhelmed by grief, I didn't think to do it."

Dez set her mouth in a line. "I'm not sure we can get a warrant for Hank Rampart's shotgun."

"I think Hank said he kept the shotgun at the cabin," Fenway said. "I bet a judge would sign off on that."

"True."

"But we might just want to ask nicely. If Hank is willing to give up his shotgun, we'll know he's less likely to be the killer."

Dez hooked her thumb over her shoulder and pointed to the interrogation room. "So Yep Younger now knows that we're looking for John Peluda, and he knows we've been able to track moves hopscotching around the county."

"I didn't see what other choice we had. And you saw his reaction. Do you think he's lying?"

"It could just be the amount of stress he's under due to the holidays," Dez said, "but he seemed like he was trying to hide his nervousness."

"All attributable to the situation we put him in," Fenway said.

"I suppose."

"How long can we leave Mr. Younger in the interrogation room?"

Dez hesitated. "We can draw things out for a little while longer. Either our deputies find the gun in his house—or they don't."

"If they do?"

"A little luminol will find blood on the shotgun even if it was cleaned," Dez said. "If they don't find the shotgun, I don't see any way around releasing him."

"Maybe you can find a few more questions to ask him. Talk to him about where he went in Peru."

Dez laughed. "You're asking me to make small talk to keep him here for—what, two hours?"

"Until the search warrant finds something."

"And what, pray tell, will *you* be doing?"

"Visiting Hank Rampart. If there's more to the story, I want to know."

CHAPTER TEN

THE LATE AFTERNOON SUN BEGAN TO SLIP BEHIND THE HILLS AS Fenway drove her Accord up the roads to the Ramparts' house. Fenway gritted her teeth—she needed to go see her father before visiting hours were over, but this was important, and there wasn't much time before Yep Younger would insist on leaving.

Fenway rang the doorbell. Barking greeted her, and she thought she could hear a man's voice say, "Bosco, quiet!"

Then silence.

Fenway waited a moment before knocking again. "Mr. Rampart, I'm so sorry to bother you, but it's Coroner Stevenson again."

A few moments later, Hank Rampart answered the door. He wore a rumpled T-shirt and bright blue sweatpants. His eyes were rimmed with red. Bosco stuck his head out between Hank's calves and sniffed.

"Again, I'm sorry to bother you, Mr. Rampart," Fenway said, "but you mentioned to Sheriff McVie that you have a shotgun."

"A Mortensen Arms twelve gauge." Hank's brow creased in confusion. "I thought that's what killed Victoria."

Fenway blinked. "I'm sorry—you think *your* shotgun killed Victoria?"

"Like I told the sheriff, we keep the shotgun in the cabin. Out there in the woods, we've had to scare off some wild animals."

"It was in the cabin when Victoria was there?"

"We taught her gun safety when she moved in with us after Rose died," Hank said. "I figured someone had broken in, found the shotgun, and killed her with it. Or maybe someone she had an argument with."

"No gun safe?"

"We don't have any children at the cabin. Top shelf of the bedroom closet. We put a lock on the closet if it's an issue, but I assume Victoria left it open."

"So you don't know where the shotgun is now?"

"I figured the police took it from the—from the crime scene." His voice caught, but he swallowed hard, then knelt down to scratch Bosco behind the ears.

Hmm. The police had searched the bedroom—the closet too, Fenway thought. No sign of the shotgun.

"When was the last time you saw the shotgun?"

"About a week ago when we were getting the cabin ready for Victoria. I made sure the shotgun was unloaded—the shells are in the nightstand drawer."

Definitely strange. The shotgun shells hadn't been there either.

"Who knew where you kept the shotgun?"

"Just me, Tricia, and Victoria."

"You've never had other guests stay at the cabin?"

"Not that we trust with the shotgun. We either keep the door locked or move the shotgun here. Too much legal liability." He sighed. "And I suppose I see why."

Fenway paused. How much should she say? "You're sure you don't know where the shotgun is now?"

Hank blinked, then looked down. "I suppose you've been talking with some of Avery's friends. Or—the people who said they were Avery's friends in high school." He squatted and scratched Bosco behind the ears.

"One or two of them, yes."

"Which lie did you hear? The one where Victoria had some stupid list of everything she hated about Avery? Or the one where Tricia and I took Victoria as a sex slave?" He stood and folded his arms. "Are you going to ask if we were angry enough to kill her or embarrassed that she might out us to the community?"

Fenway was quiet.

He shook his head. "The only ones I'm angry at are those supposed friends of hers. Victoria was like a daughter to us."

Bosco flopped onto his side, and Hank bent down again and scratched his belly.

"I don't want to relive this, Coroner. It wasn't easy, but we don't have any reason to want Victoria dead."

Fenway nodded. "I appreciate you telling me that." She looked at his face—his eyes were open and direct. She took her phone out. "We also discovered a piece of paper in Victoria's trailer at the studio lot where they were rehearsing for the Christmas parade." Fenway showed Hank the picture of the letters and the five-digit numbers. "Does this mean anything to you?"

$L - 32230$

$P - 85077$

$StL - 77104$

$K - 15248$

$D - 93415$

Hank pointed to the $P - 85077$. "That one is Rose Ellen's old zip code in Phoenix. We had to fill out a bunch of legal paperwork when we became Victoria's guardians." He pointed to the last number. "That's an Estancia zip code. The others, I don't know. I guess that one is St. Louis, but it doesn't mean anything to me."

"Did Victoria say anything about searching for her missing birth father?"

"Besides the fact that he owed her and her mom a million dollars?" Hank shook his head. "Every so often, she'd say she had a lead on where he was. But then she'd drop it for a few months."

"Why did she come out here?"

"She said the Christmas parade was a good opportunity to expand her brand," Hank said. "Truthfully, I don't think that was it. I think she wanted to come see us, but maybe she didn't want to impose."

"What makes you say that?"

"First of all, the Estancia Christmas Parade is just a local thing. Yes, our local celebrities have fun with it, and Ferris Energy puts a bunch of money into making it look like the Rose Parade instead of a small-town mom-and-pop parade, but for anyone with a following like Victoria, this parade is a waste of time." Hank looked over his shoulder, then leaned forward. "And when Victoria came over for dinner, she left her phone on the table when she went to get more wine. An email came through acknowledging that Victoria had turned down a live Christmas Eve cooking show for the Red & Rosé channel. That's got a national audience. You don't turn that down for the Estancia Christmas Parade unless you have a personal reason."

"So," Fenway said carefully, "if she had found her real father living in Estancia..."

Hank stopped scratching Bosco's head. "Huh. Well, maybe coming to see us wasn't the only reason she wanted to visit Estancia."

"Do you have any idea who Victoria's father might be?"

Hank slowly shook his head. "I know his name was John Peluda —Victoria showed me the legal paperwork. After Victoria and Avery became friends, I asked a private detective friend of mine to track Peluda down. He ran some cursory stuff but didn't find anything. He said he'd need a lot more money to do a full investigation. And by then, Victoria would be eighteen. Tricia and I figured we'd throw our energy into helping her with the here and now rather than trying to track down a guy who might have died a month after that original judgment was handed down—or who might have left the country."

"I see." Fenway cleared her throat. "You know, sometimes, kids can share more personal details with one parental figure than the other. Any chance Tricia might know something about John Peluda that you don't?"

"It's possible," Hank said, "but Tricia is in no shape to answer questions. She took something to calm her down a little while ago, and she's sleeping."

Fenway nodded. "Thanks for your time, Mr. Rampart. And again, I'm so sorry for your loss."

His eyes lost focus. "It's like losing Avery all over again." He snapped back into himself, nodded at Fenway, and closed the door, Bosco whining.

Fenway walked back to the Accord parked on the street and unlocked the car.

If what Hank had been saying was true and the murder weapon had been in the cabin, that changed things.

Did the killer have time to get the shotgun from the closet and the shells from the nightstand, then load it?

Obviously, they must have. Which meant that Victoria knew her killer.

No—there was another possibility. Victoria could have thought there was a threat, gotten the shotgun, loaded it herself, and then perhaps been overpowered by her assailant.

Either way, it was possible that the killer hadn't intended to kill Victoria when they arrived. An argument, perhaps. Or a burglar who'd intended to steal from the cabin and didn't expect to find Victoria there.

Fenway pinched the bridge of her nose in thought. Then what was Victoria doing in the bedroom? If she'd surprised a burglar, would she have been sitting at her desk? No—from her position, it was most likely that she was working on her laptop, then stood up in surprise before taking the shotgun blast to the face.

She unlocked the Accord and got in.

Her phone rang in her purse.

"Hi, Dez."

"Deputy Salvador just found Yep Younger's shotgun in his back-yard behind a tool shed. Recently fired, blood spatter on the barrel. I arrested Mr. Younger for murder about five minutes ago."

CHAPTER ELEVEN

THE WIND TURNED COLD AS FENWAY OPENED THE DOOR OF THE
Accord in the dark parking lot of St. Vincent's Hospital. She
opened the trunk. A light-blue Western Washington sweatshirt was
in a short cardboard box, and Fenway took it out and pulled it over
her blouse. It wouldn't win any fashion awards, but at least she'd be
warm.

She walked as quickly as she could across the parking lot and
into the hospital, then waited at the nurses' station to sign into the
intensive care unit.

As she walked down the linoleum-floored corridors toward the
ICU, her feet dragged. She passed the gift shop, full of Christmas
balloons and poinsettias, stuffed reindeer, and greeting cards
covered in red and green. She was bone tired.

She'd never really enjoyed the Christmas season; it had always
been just her and her mom, and the first year in Seattle, they'd been
too poor to have a tree. Fenway got a stocking filled with inexpen-
sive chocolates and a couple of small notebooks. Santa brought her
a cheap colored pen set and two paperback books. She'd given her

mother a sculpture she'd made at school—a cat that didn't really look like a cat.

She remembered all the gifts she got from Santa the previous year, when they had been living in luxury with her rich father in Estancia. A new bike. A large, intricate dollhouse she didn't really want. A video game system. Two huge, beautiful stuffed animals.

That was the Christmas she realized that Santa wasn't real— that it was her mom wrapping gifts and putting "From Santa" on it. And in her slanted, loopy cursive, too. Fenway remembered looking at the tag on the wrapping of the paperbacks and recognizing her mother's handwriting in the "S" of Santa.

The day after Christmas, nine-year-old Fenway had accompanied her mother to a clearance sale, where they got a three-foot-tall fake tree and a box of heavily discounted ornaments, as well as a string of tinsel. That was the tree they had until Fenway left to go to Western Washington.

At the threshold to her father's intensive care room, she saw Nathaniel Ferris lying supine in the hospital bed, an oxygen tube in his nose but no movement in his limbs or face, no rapid eye movement under his lids.

For once, Charlotte wasn't there.

She pulled out her phone and looked at her messages. She'd missed one from Charlotte:

After the board meeting today I need to get some last-minute Christmas shopping done
I saw your father at lunch so I will just come early tomorrow
Let's talk about Christmas Day later

With Charlotte gone, Fenway could continue to read to her father. She dug in her purse and pulled out the increasingly dog-eared paperback by the South African comedian that was on the bestseller list.

She started at chapter eleven, where she'd left off a couple of days before. She read the first paragraph—then it hit her.

Fenway hadn't yet purchased a Christmas gift for her father. The realization felt like a punch in the gut. Why hadn't she bought his gift yet?

Did she believe he would never wake up?

The day after her father had gotten out of surgery, the doctors had said he'd wake up any day now. A week later: any day now. A week after that: any day now.

Still, when she asked: any day now.

But she was asking less and less frequently. And so was Charlotte.

It had only been—what, seven weeks? But she saw the loss of muscle definition in Nathaniel Ferris's arms and legs, and even his face was thinner.

He probably wouldn't wake up before Christmas—not when there were only two days left. This would not only be her first Christmas without her mother, but it would be without either of her parents.

When she'd moved out of her mother's house in Seattle, packing like crazy for two weeks straight, she'd come across the three-foot cheap Christmas tree in the garage, and she'd thrown it away.

Now, she wished she'd kept it.

Her apartment was empty of Christmas decorations, and her office was, too. Migs had asked why Fenway didn't have any holiday décor up, and Fenway mumbled something about her father being in the hospital, which was true.

But so far, even with the budding romance with McVie, her world was on pause.

She was waiting for her father to wake up.

But more than that—she was waiting for her mother to come back. To be able to see her again. Ask her advice. Even hear her deep, steady breaths as she slept in the next room.

And she would never hear that again.

Fenway cleared her throat and read the next paragraph aloud, not paying attention to the words on the page.

———

An hour later, Fenway walked out of the hospital. It was dark. She should call McVie. Two days before Christmas—had she ever been anything but single over the holidays before? A few summer flings, but nothing over Christmas. Nothing serious enough to spend time at the other's house, anyway.

She pulled her phone out of her purse, and her finger hovered over the screen.

Ugh. She didn't want to go over to McVie's. She didn't want him coming over to her apartment tonight, either.

Why not?

He was attentive, he could make her laugh, he was—well, he was good-looking. Not that it was important to spend the holidays with him just because he was attractive. But it didn't hurt.

What was wrong with her?

She arrived at her car, unlocked the door, and sat in the driver's seat without turning the car on.

Victoria Versini had come to Estancia to find her father. To make him pay—literally. A daughter who'd been abandoned by her father, who had to research his whereabouts to get him to finally take responsibility for—

A twinge in Fenway's neck.

She saw her father's face, contorted, in the courtroom almost two months before. *No wonder you hate me. No wonder you feel like I didn't do anything for you.*

But her father hadn't abandoned her. He'd taken a bullet for her, in fact.

Victoria, though—Victoria was different. Her father *had* abandoned her. And if their theory of the crime was correct, when

Victoria found her father and confronted him, instead of welcoming her with open arms, he killed her.

Almost a million dollars. People had killed for less.

But Fenway's father, when he realized the money for Fenway's college hadn't ever made it into her account, pulled his checkbook out and wrote a check out—a six-figure check—on the spot.

She felt empty. She'd spent the last two decades of her life being angry at her father when he hadn't abandoned her like she'd thought.

But Victoria Versini was a different story. She'd grown up struggling just as much as Fenway had, and they'd both lost their mothers to cancer. But when Fenway's mother died, Nathaniel Ferris had pulled strings to get her an apartment, a job—a new life. Victoria had to move in with her friend's family. They were both lucky enough to go to college, get a good-paying job.

Fenway felt a drip on her trousers and realized she had tears running down her face.

She tapped her phone.

I'm not coming over tonight

She sent the message to McVie, then waited. Three dots appeared, then vanished. Then appeared again, this time for a few more seconds, then disappeared again.

Fenway felt the bottom drop out of her stomach. It wouldn't be fair to give McVie no explanation at all. But she didn't want to talk about it. She didn't think she could keep it together, not with her father fighting for his life in a coma, and not while trying to get justice for a woman who could have traded places with Fenway under different circumstances.

She held the phone in her hand, then sighed and tapped again.

Sorry

She put the phone in her cupholder, turned the car on, and backed out of her parking space.

———

Fenway's apartment offered little respite. No Christmas decorations, of course. Did that make her feel better because it wasn't reminding her of her first Christmas without her mother, or worse because she wasn't even acknowledging the holiday?

She spent a few minutes pacing around her small apartment, opening the refrigerator and deciding she wasn't hungry. She looked at her bookshelf, but she didn't want to read.

She called Dez's cell phone.

"Fenway?"

"Did Younger say anything?"

"Called his lawyer. He's being arraigned tomorrow. I'm at home."

"Oh—sorry. I guess you would be."

"You should go home too."

"And the paperwork can wait till tomorrow morning," Fenway said, then stifled a yawn.

"No, ma'am," Dez said. "Evidence report is on your desk."

"Oh, look at you, trying to impress your boss." Fenway chuckled. "Did we get an arraignment time?"

"Nine fifteen. Court's closing at noon."

"Sounds good," Fenway said. "The shotgun's in the evidence room?"

"Handed it in myself."

"Excellent." Fenway thought for a moment. "Younger said he had a Blue Heron, right? I hear the barrel has a touch of blue if you see it in the right light. Is that true?"

Dez paused. "A Blue Heron?"

"Yeah, he said that's what his dad's shotgun was."

"This wasn't a Blue Heron. It was a Mortensen Arms."

Fenway drew in a breath.

"That's not Younger's shotgun?"

"No," Fenway said, "you weren't in the room when he said his shotgun was a Blue Heron?"

Dez grunted. "Younger's shotgun isn't registered in the state of California, so I didn't have anything to check it against when I ran the paperwork." A sharp smacking sound—perhaps Dez had hit a table or a counter with an open hand. "I swear, these lobbyists who are against a national database—"

"Right, right—but this doesn't necessarily get Younger off the hook." Fenway paced back and forth from her bedroom to her kitchen. "He could have killed her with a shotgun he found and then panicked and taken it with him."

"If it's not Younger's shotgun, then whose is it?" Dez clicked her tongue. "And where would he have found a shotgun?"

"Hold on a second." Fenway walked back to the kitchen and got her notebook out of her purse, then flipped several pages before she found the interview notes from Henry Rampart. "You said the shotgun you found is a Mortensen Arms?"

"Yes. The twelve gauge."

"I think that's Hank Rampart's shotgun. It's the one he says he left in the cabin for Victoria to protect herself."

"Then," Dez said, "you think Mr. Younger found it at the cabin?"

Fenway frowned. Hank Rampart had convinced her that the rumors about Victoria weren't true—that neither he nor Tricia wanted Victoria dead. She shut her eyes. Was this really about Victoria's father?

"Okay, let's think about this. Victoria finds out that Yep Younger is her father. She confronts him somehow."

"But that wouldn't have been at her cabin, would it?"

"Unlikely, I agree. The cabin's in the middle of nowhere. No, I expect that Victoria would have gone to his artichoke farm. Or maybe had coffee with him in a public place."

"Any evidence that happened?"

Fenway sighed. "We didn't check any of the tire tracks at the artichoke farm. Maybe the Alfa Romeo Spyder uses a unique set of tires."

"We can get CSI—or heck, even one of the deputies—to go check out any tires or tire marks."

"I hate to have one of them do it tonight."

"The Alfa was towed to the impound yard—no one has to drive up into the hills."

"But the tire tracks at the farm—and it's been at least two days since Victoria Versini would have visited."

"Better than nothing, right?"

"I suppose. Even better would be getting Victoria Versini's phone records."

"The wireless carrier can't process that request until after Christmas."

"After Christmas? It's usually a twenty-four-hour turnaround!"

"Not at the holidays. That department is short-staffed this week and next. Besides, two business days is well within the established parameters. And they didn't ask for a warrant, which they could have."

Fenway scoffed. "Which they never had regarding a murder victim before."

"Even so, you might have a supervisor who's a stickler," Dez said. "Okay—since it's dark, I'll have Celeste or Brian go up to the farm first thing tomorrow and take pictures of the tire tracks in the dirt lot there. But after three days, I wouldn't hold my breath."

"I've never been this glad for lack of rain before. Now it might keep our tire tracks preserved."

"And I'll go to the impound yard myself to take comparison photos of the Alfa."

"Did CSI find anything in the Alfa itself?"

"Registration, owner's manual, an empty soda can, a jacket in the back seat. Nothing in the trunk, and no papers besides the car information." Dez hesitated. "Are you okay?"

"I'm fine," Fenway said automatically. "Well—I don't know. I guess this case is hitting a little close to home."

Dez was quiet for a moment. Then: "Do you want to talk about it?"

"Not really."

"Okay. I wasn't in the courtroom last month, but I know it was intense, so if you need to blow off some steam—"

"Thanks," Fenway said quickly. "I appreciate it. But I'm okay." Then after a few seconds: "Really."

"If you say so," Dez said.

PART 3

CHRISTMAS EVE

CHAPTER TWELVE

At Java Jim's, Fenway leaned against the wall next to the pastry case, holding Dez's large coffee, and waited for her latte. She blinked several times rapidly to get her eyes to focus. Her shoulder was sore from tossing and turning most of the night.

Her phone buzzed in her purse. She took it out—McVie had texted her.

R u up for bfast? Jack and Jills my treat

She texted back.

Sorry Dez and I are heading to impound yard to check out Victoria's Alfa

The barista called out "Joanne," and Fenway stepped forward to claim her drink.

"Can I get you a drink carrier?"

Fenway shook her head. "Just walking across the plaza."

The latte was hot, and Fenway's fingers started burning even through the cardboard sleeve. She gritted her teeth and walked across the dark plaza to her office building. She opened the front door with difficulty and had to set the coffees down on the floor in front of the coroner's office suite to pull her keys out of her purse. She should have gotten the drink carrier.

Dez wasn't in yet, so Fenway set the coffees on the counter in front of the empty administrative assistant's desk. Rachel's backfill had finally been approved, and she'd narrowed the candidate list down considerably. It was always tough to fill positions around the holidays, but she had a couple of interviews in the week after Christmas.

Her phone buzzed again.

do u want 2 come over tonite
we can leave out milk & cookies for santa

Fenway rolled her eyes. Spending Christmas morning with McVie would be good, she supposed—and she'd get to spend part of the day with him before going to the mansion to spend a sad, lonely Christmas dinner with Charlotte—and before McVie had to go spend Christmas dinner with Amy and her rich new husband.

Dez opened the door to the coroner's suite.

"You're bright eyed and bushy tailed this morning," Dez grunted.

Fenway pushed the large coffee over. "After I found out that Celeste had the day off, I figured I'd go with you to the impound yard."

Dez picked up the cup and took a long sip, then looked out of the corner of her eye at Fenway as if to say, *Has this case affected you that much, Fenway? Or is this just an excuse to avoid something you don't want to deal with?*

Fenway supposed it could be both.

"I think there's something we're missing," Fenway said. "All the evidence points to Yep Younger, it's true, but I'm having trouble piecing together how he might have done it—and how he found out about the judgment against him. A lot of things don't make sense."

"Crimes don't always get neatly wrapped up with a bow," Dez said. "Sometimes killers have motives that only make sense to themselves. I mean—not to speak unkindly of the man, but Yep Younger is obsessed with artichokes. You saw how his eyes lit up when he talked about cross-breeding the Peruvian artichokes with the California ones."

"The Salamanca artichokes with the green globes."

"All right, you don't need to show off, Miss Foodie." Dez took another sip of the coffee. "Are you ready?"

Fenway and Dez walked out of the coroner's building and across the street to the sheriff's office. The entry greeted them with red and green light strands hung up behind the front desk, as well as a barrel filled to the top with unwrapped toys.

"Nice to see the toy drive do so well."

"It was better when Alice Jenkins was mayor," Dez said. "We'd have one of these barrels on every floor, just as full as this one. Mayor Jenkins used to do community outreach starting just after Thanksgiving."

They walked through the corridors of the building, past McVie's empty office. Fenway noticed that the clock on the wall of the bullpen read just a few minutes past six thirty. "We'd need to go through their financials to be sure, but I can't imagine a small farm like that could absorb a million-dollar judgment."

"I wish Piper were still here. She'd be able to weasel her way into Diamond Hill's financials—and find a legal way to do it, too."

Dez opened the back door into the lot where the cruisers were kept. "We can look into how the business is structured. If it's a sole proprietorship, things can get messy—and yes, the business money could potentially be used to pay off the judgment against the owner. But if it's an LLC or an S corp, Younger can't use the money from the business to pay off his debt." She took keys out of her pocket and opened the cruiser in the third parking space from the door.

Fenway furrowed her brow as she and Dez got in. "I agree—he couldn't do it *legally*. But I bet there's some loophole to exploit, or he could pay himself some sort of million-dollar bonus. But after seeing how much he loves what he does, I'm not sure he *would*. If he had to choose between personal financial ruin and destroying his business—"

"Then he'd choose option three." Dez started the engine. "And get rid of the threat."

They drove out of the lot, turning down Fifth Street away from the freeway. "But that assumes that he *intended* to kill her," Fenway said. "And that would mean he'd take his Blue Heron shotgun with him to the cabin."

"Unless," Dez said, "he went there with the intention of negotiating with her. Maybe she stands firm—a million dollars. Maybe she says something he doesn't like."

"But when I spoke with Hank Rampart," Fenway said, "he told me he doesn't keep the shotgun loaded."

Dez turned down Santa Magdalena Avenue. "You think anyone would admit to keeping a loaded shotgun at the cabin after knowing what happened there?" She crinkled her nose. "He might have even convinced himself that he kept the gun unloaded—sort of a defense mechanism against the guilt he felt."

Fenway was quiet.

"The shotgun we found yesterday won't get processed until later today—or maybe even after Christmas," Dez said. "The blood evidence—I think we can assume it's Victoria's, but the lab is backed up. We'll be lucky to get a positive match by Valentine's Day."

"If Yep Younger did it," Fenway said, "it would have to be a crime of opportunity, right?"

Dez considered for a moment. "Maybe Victoria invited Yep to the cabin to ask him to do a Photoxio post with her—you know, here's the guy who grows the best artichokes in America—and then when he gets there, she hits him with the judgment. Tells him that he has to pay her a million bucks. He goes crazy, grabs the gun, and kills her." Dez scratched her head. "That would explain why the laptop was open."

"The camera wasn't set up," Fenway said. "The camera and the ring light were in a bag next to the bed."

Dez drummed her fingers on the steering wheel. "Isn't there a built-in camera on the laptop?"

"You think Victoria would ever record a Photoxio video without her professional camera and ring light?"

"But if she only intended to confront Younger—"

Fenway set her mouth in a line. "Yes, it's possible, I'll give you that."

On the next block, a high chain-link fence with barbed wire at the top appeared on the right-hand side. Dez turned into a gated driveway halfway down the block, then flashed her badge to the guard who stepped out of the booth.

"Morning, Sergeant Roubideaux," the guard said. "Merry Christmas."

"Merry Christmas to you too, Pete," Dez said. "You know Coroner Stevenson?"

"I voted for her," Pete said, bending down, his hands on his knees. "We've got the Alfa Romeo you were asking about in garage 3A. Let me know if you need anything." He gave Fenway a half-nod. "Nice to meet you."

"Likewise."

Pete stood and went back to his guard station, pushed a button, and the orange-and-white gate arm raised. Dez drove the cruiser in over the pockmarked asphalt, then turned left. A set of garages appeared on the left, and Dez stopped the car and killed the engine.

"3A?" Fenway asked, opening the door.

Dez nodded.

The darkness of the early morning was slipping into a dank gray light. The impound yard smelled of engine oil with a touch of the unpleasant scent of ironwood. As Fenway walked toward the garage, two harsh bright lights, mounted on tall wooden poles on either side of the garage building, came on.

Dez stepped up to a roll-up door marked 3A and uncovered a keypad next to the door. She punched in a number, and a mechanical whir announced the door going up.

Victoria Versini's candy-apple-red Alfa Romeo Spyder sat inside, its convertible top closed. Dez turned on the lights in the garage, and the fluorescent lights reflected off the shiny paint, giving it a surreal, almost sterile quality.

Fenway knelt next to the front tire.

"Pincellani Century Three-Sixties," Fenway said. "Not a super-common tire. I think we could get a tread match if the dirt lot at Diamond Hill Farms hasn't been messed up too much."

"What size?"

Fenway squinted. "Looks like 175—uh, is that a seventy or a DO?"

"It's a seventy."

"70VR15."

Dez nodded and pulled out her phone. "We can get that pulled up from the database. But take pictures of the tread anyway—we can get a better idea of the tire from the tread wear."

"There's a tire tread database?" Fenway took three pictures of the tread of the front left tire, then stood.

"Has been for a couple of years now." Dez looked sideways at Fenway. "Didn't they teach you all about the tire tread database in that fancy grad program of yours?"

"Just because I took the class last year doesn't mean they created the curriculum last year."

"True." Dez turned back to the Spyder. "So was that worth coming all the way out here and getting up early?"

"You don't want to search the car?"

"CSI has already been over it."

"I know—but now that we know that Victoria was trying to find her father, maybe we should take another look."

Dez sighed. "Fine. But I want to get to Diamond Hill Farms in the next half hour. You have ten minutes."

Fenway got a pair of blue nitrile gloves from her purse and opened the driver's-side door. She felt around under the seat and lifted the soda can out of the cup holder.

"Anything?" Dez asked.

"Not yet." Fenway walked around to the passenger's-side door, opened it, then knelt down to look under the seat.

"Four minutes." Dez walked around the car and stood over Fenway.

Fenway found nothing under the seat on the passenger's side, but when she lifted the floor mat, something felt off. She pulled the floor mat up and looked at the plastic liner on the bottom. Nothing —but she heard a crinkle. She bent the plastic liner and it separated slightly from the rest of the floor mat. A piece of paper was stuck to in the gap.

"What's that?"

"I don't know," Fenway replied, pulling the paper out of the gap. "CSI didn't log this, did they?"

"I didn't see it in the report."

Fenway stood and unfolded the paper. On the plain white sheet, it said:

Mr. Younger,

Thirty-one years ago, you got a woman named Ellen Rose Johnson pregnant in Arizona. She was my mother, and I have conclusively determined that you are the father. A judge in Arizona has determined that you owe my mother and me for eighteen years of child support. I'd like to discuss this with you as soon as possible. Meet me at my cabin on December 21 at 10 P.M.

Sincerely,

Vicki Versini

Fenway pulled her phone out and took a picture of the letter, then scrolled to the picture of the list with the zip codes.

L – 32230
P – 85077
StL – 77104
K – 15248
D – 93415

Fenway pointed at *December 21* on the paper. "Look at that."

Dez squinted. "December 21?"

"Look at the 'D' in the list. It doesn't look like the 'D' in 'December.'"

"So the list might not have been made by Victoria Versini after all?"

Fenway nodded. "I suppose it might have been a list by a private investigator, or maybe it was just a random piece of paper that Victoria had in her possession. For all we know, it could be a list that one of her ex-boyfriends made that she couldn't bear to part with. Or maybe a secret lover she had, and they communicated in code."

"Or maybe she's a secret agent," Dez said.

"Okay—granted, those aren't likely scenarios, but I'm trying to figure out why the handwriting doesn't match."

Dez pointed to the *21*. "The '2' could have been written by the same hand. The curves are the same."

"But the 'D' is different."

Dez's forehead crinkled. "People write differently when they're writing a letter versus writing a list." She looked up at Fenway. "Besides—we don't know what the letters and numbers mean yet. We're operating under the assumption that they're zip codes and that Victoria Versini was using them to track down her birth father, but we don't have hard evidence for that. It seems to be the most likely explanation, but we don't have all the information."

"True enough." Fenway stood. "We should get this into evidence. Would you get a baggie from my purse?"

"Sure." Dez rummaged in Fenway's bag and held out an evidence baggie.

"And with two minutes to spare," Fenway said, putting the letter inside.

CHAPTER THIRTEEN

DEZ STOPPED THE CRUISER ON THE SIDE OF THE ROAD, ABOUT twenty feet in front of the turnoff onto the dirt road to Diamond Hill Artichokes. She and Fenway got out and walked to the beginning of the dirt road.

"Do you see tracks that look like a match?" Dez asked.

Fenway pulled up the tire photo on her phone. "It's hard to tell. Not a lot of visible tire treads. The dirt's tightly packed here. Maybe further up the road."

Dez sucked in air through her teeth. "It's public property here. It's a business, open to the public, so the law is usually clear that we can go wherever the public can and collect evidence. But a good lawyer could argue that we'd need a warrant if we want to take photos of the tire tracks."

"But Younger already had us visit this property. He invited us in to look at his gun safe."

Dez tilted her head. "Yes, I know—and I suppose that's why I wanted to get here and get out before the artichoke store opened. I suppose there are workers out in the fields already." She pointed to three vehicles in the lot: two older-model pickup trucks, and one five- or six-year-old Hyundai.

"If anyone comes, let's just say we need to speak with Marla Quiñones. We'll ask her if she's seen Yep Younger's shotgun. I know it's not relevant to the investigation, but it's still missing. If someone stole the shotgun, that could pose a danger to the community."

"We can do that."

They walked up the hill of the dirt driveway, and as it flattened out, a tire tread caught Fenway's eye.

"That looks like the Pincellani tread," she said. "See the two sets of slight diagonals on those two vertical sections and the S-curve on the outside?"

Dez furrowed her brow. "That looks similar, yeah, but this looks a lot wider than the tires on Victoria's Alfa."

Fenway looked at the tread on her phone and at the tread mark in the dirt. "It's definitely a Pincellani," she said, taking a picture of the tire track. "And those aren't very common tires. They come standard on a few expensive luxury cars, and you can buy them, of course, but only people like Victoria Versini have them."

"And your father," Dez said—and caught herself.

Fenway nodded and turned away. Yes, her father's Porsche 911S probably had Pincellani tires. She forced her attention back to the dirt parking lot.

The wide Pincellani tire tracks went up to a heavily trafficked area in front of the outbuilding where the tractors had been parked two days before. She swept the area as she'd been taught to do in her forensics classes, slow and steady. Every so often, she glanced up at Dez, who was doing the same thing on the other side of the dirt lot.

She found the tire track again around the side of the lot, as it probably turned around before leaving. But a narrower Pincellani tread was nowhere to be found. "Any luck, Dez?"

"Nothing."

Fenway looked down at the ground; she'd already gone over that area. "I don't think Victoria was here. Or if she was, the dirt's been disturbed so much, the tracks have been completely covered up."

"I figured we'd get *something*," Dez said. "It rained the night before Victoria was killed, so I figured we'd get some good tracks if she came here the day she died."

"Maybe she came before it rained."

"It's possible."

Fenway turned to go back down the hill toward the cruiser. "Where to now?"

"We need to enter the letter into evidence."

"What about the stolen Blue Heron shotgun?"

Dez followed Fenway down the hill. "Right now, it's just missing, not stolen. If Yep Younger wants to file a police report, that's up to him. For all we know, he's got it at his house."

"Right." Fenway paused. "Do you need to be at the arraignment?"

"That's not until nine fifteen."

"It's eight thirty."

"What?" Dez shook her head. "I didn't realize it would take us so long to cover the parking lot. All right—can you log in the evidence while I head over to the courthouse?"

"Sure."

They drove back to City Hall in silence. Finally, Dez spoke.

"How's your father doing?"

Fenway blinked a few times. "Same."

"Do the doctors have any other ideas?"

Fenway shook her head.

A few beats of silence.

"Charlotte's taking it hard," Fenway said. "She's working on keeping Ferris Energy afloat—a bunch of high-level people have quit. So that's keeping her busy. But with the company offices closed today and tomorrow, she's got nothing to do but think about my dad."

"And how are you doing?"

Fenway shrugged. "Fine."

Dez glanced at Fenway but said nothing.

————

Fenway entered the letter into the evidence room, then came back to the coroner's office suite. McVie was waiting for her with an extra-large Java Jim's cup.

"Hey, you," he said.

"How long have you been here?"

"About five minutes. I saw you at the entrance to the evidence room, and I finally finished up my paperwork on that string of robberies, so I figured you could use a mid-morning pick-me-up." He handed the cup to her. "Extra-large latte."

"Thanks." Fenway took a long drink; it was still hot, but not scorching.

"So are you free for lunch?"

Fenway frowned. "I mean, I am, but I'm kind of distracted with the case."

"What's going on?"

She told McVie about the letter she had found in Victoria Versini's car, as well as the Pincellani tires: the narrower ones on Versini's Alfa Romeo and the wide ones she found in the dirt lot at the artichoke farm.

"Lots of cars have Pincellani tires," McVie said. "Sure, they're limited to luxury cars for the most part, but you'd be surprised at how many people have them in this area."

"Dez was saying there's a tire tread database?"

"Right," McVie said. "Matches any tire tread with the make and model of the tire. Pretty quick too. It's an automated system—used to be DVDs they sent around to all the law enforcement agencies. Now it's all cloud-based; just upload the photo and submit it, and you'll have a match—or a couple of likely matches—within twenty-four hours."

"Then we can check out who ordered them."

"And you'll be able to cross-reference which new cars are sold with that type of tire as standard equipment, too. A DMV search will be quicker than going through financial records of all the tire stores in the county."

"If the tires were even sold in the county."

"Right."

"And all this will tell us is if someone drove into that lot. They could have been buying artichokes, or they could have been a salesperson for some new fancy artichoke harvester. We were thinking it would be Victoria's Alfa Romeo, but it's definitely not that. This seems like a wild goose chase—and besides, there were plenty of other tire tracks there that we *didn't* take pictures of."

"Do you want to submit it to the tire tread database or not?"

"I guess so," Fenway said. "I should learn how to use it anyway."

"You're gonna love the database," McVie said. "It's pretty cool."

They went into Fenway's office, and she docked her laptop, then McVie pulled a second chair around behind Fenway's desk and showed her the database. Within half an hour, Fenway had uploaded the photos and received an email confirmation that her report would be ready by the next morning.

"Not really the kind of Christmas present I wanted," Fenway said, "but it'll do."

"Speaking of which," McVie said. "Do you want to open our presents Christmas Eve or Christmas morning?"

Fenway looked at McVie. "Christmas morning. Doesn't everyone?"

He shook his head. "Growing up, my family would always open them Christmas Eve. Only Santa gave his gifts on Christmas morning."

A flash in Fenway's mind to the secondhand paperbacks she

received. Not a lot of opportunities to unwrap multiple gifts when she was growing up.

"So you want to open our gifts tonight?"

He shrugged. "Amy's family always opened theirs Christmas morning, so I just went with it. Made it easy around the holidays at first. I'd go over to my parents' house and open gifts with them on Christmas Eve."

Fenway didn't really want to talk about how McVie spent his Christmases with his ex. "We can do it tonight. That's fine." Fenway glanced at the clock on her phone. "Yep Younger is getting arraigned as we speak."

McVie nodded. "Dez is there, right?"

"Correct." She paused. "I know we're going where the evidence takes us, but I'm positive we're missing something."

"The shotgun in Younger's yard is pretty damning."

"But it's not even his shotgun."

McVie's eyebrows knotted. "What do you mean, it's not his shotgun?"

"I thought Dez would have told you. Yep Younger had his father's shotgun—it was a Blue Heron twelve gauge. But the shotgun found on Younger's property was a Mortensen Arms. Henry Rampart said that he kept a Mortensen Arms shotgun in the cabin since it was out in the middle of nowhere—you know, protection against mountain lions and other wild animals."

McVie frowned. "Henry Rampart told you this?"

"Right."

He leaned back in his chair and rubbed his chin. "So you're uneasy because of what Henry Rampart told you?"

"Partially, I suppose." Fenway paused. "I mean, the letter addressed to Yep Younger clearly gives him motive. But—why was it found in Victoria's car and not somewhere at Younger's work or house?"

"Maybe she gave the letter to Younger and he read it, refused to believe it, and threw it back at her."

"Maybe." She paused. "What are you thinking?"

"When we base assumptions off what witnesses say, sometimes we don't take into account that those witnesses could be suspects—or even if they're not, they could have their own agendas."

"I assure you, we have," Fenway said. "We think Henry Rampart feels guilty about leaving a loaded shotgun in the cabin. If he had done what the law recommends and kept the ammunition separate from the gun, Victoria wouldn't have been murdered."

"What if there's another reason?" McVie asked.

"Another reason?"

"Yes. What if Henry Rampart murdered Victoria himself?"

Fenway blinked. "Why would he do that?"

"I saw your interview notes with one of Victoria's former high school classmates."

"Kendra Chanticleer—yes. Not the biggest fan of Victoria."

"Victoria was a bully in high school, if I'm not mistaken."

"Kendra certainly thought so."

"Is this an opinion shared by others in the class or just Kendra?"

Fenway paused. "I—I don't know. I haven't interviewed anyone else."

"Brian Callahan went to high school with Victoria—and the Ramparts' daughter, Avery, too. He saw what case we were working on and voiced his opinion about her—and it was much the same as Kendra's. She was a bully—to just about everyone, including her friends."

Fenway felt a tug in her heart. "She'd just lost her mother—"

McVie held up his hand. "I'm not asking you to make excuses for her. But remember how Avery died?"

Fenway folded her arms and nodded.

"Now suppose," McVie said, "Henry Rampart found something. Or maybe Victoria said something on this visit."

"I actually—" Fenway bit her lip, then looked up at McVie. "I heard that Victoria made a list of stuff she hated about Avery, and everyone saw it." She pursed her lips. "You also heard Jack Dragon insinuate that Hank and Tricia had a physically intimate relationship with Victoria."

"So maybe—"

"Hank Rampart says the rumors aren't true," she said.

"And you believe him?"

Fenway leaned her elbows on her desk and rested her head in her hands. "I do, yes. Why would the Ramparts wait this long to get their revenge on Victoria, anyway? Wouldn't they have kicked her out after Avery's suicide? Not paid for Victoria's college? What about getting Victoria her big break? Were they just playing the long game?"

McVie rubbed his chin. "Maybe some fact came to light that changed everything." He leaned forward in his chair. "Everyone says that Victoria wouldn't have taken this job for the money or the exposure. Too small potatoes. There has to be another reason—and we thought it was to find her father. But what if it was to apologize to Hank and Tricia—who had let her into their home—for being a bully to Avery? Or what if Henry had found one of Avery's old diaries, detailing all the mean things Victoria had said to her?"

"He might think that Victoria was responsible for Avery's death."

McVie nodded. "We don't have any evidence for that—only the hint that Victoria was a bully. But don't base a theory of the case on what Henry Rampart told you. He has every reason to lie—either to protect himself or Tricia. So he would *seem* like a guilt-ridden father figure, and he wouldn't look like someone with a reason to want Victoria dead."

Fenway was silent for a moment.

McVie rubbed his chin. "I wish we knew what those letters and zip codes meant."

"Here's what I think we should do," Fenway said. "I say we go back to the cabin. Now that we know where Henry Rampart *said* the shotgun was, maybe we can walk through some of the scenarios we've thought of."

McVie nodded. "See if anything seems out of place—maybe even come up with a theory of how Younger—or someone else —did it."

"I suppose we could look for tire tracks at the cabin, too."

"See?" McVie said. "I *told* you that you were gonna love the tire tread database."

CHAPTER FOURTEEN

THIS TIME, FENWAY WAS WATCHING FOR THE DIP IN THE ROAD TO the cabin—and it still surprised her when McVie drove straight onto the gravel driveway. She felt her stomach drop.

"Sorry," McVie said from the driver's seat. "I tried to go slower that time."

"It's fine."

They pulled to a stop in the gravel driveway, and McVie killed the engine.

Fenway got out of the Highlander and took a look around the front of the cabin—something she hadn't done the first time she'd been there. She walked over to a yellowish-brown stain in a section of the gravel in front of the hedge. She pointed to it. "This is the brake fluid?"

"Correct. And CSI is certain the hose had been cut."

Fenway walked around the edge of the driveway, looking for where the gravel met the dirt.

"Tire tracks?"

Fenway pointed. "There's a Pincellani tire mark here. It's narrow, like the one from Victoria's Alfa Romeo." She pulled her phone out, then knelt down, comparing the tire mark on the ground to the tread of the Spyder's tire in the photo. "I guess the database could say for sure, but it passes the eyeball test."

"That makes sense. She'd been staying here for a couple of days."

Fenway continued to walk slowly around the perimeter of the driveway, but she found nothing else.

"Hey," McVie said, motioning her over to the carport. "Look at this."

The area under the carport was a concrete pad, and clear tire marks stretched across it.

Fenway shook her head. "Those aren't Pincellani tires. More like a Capstone or maybe a Mannavie."

"Right," McVie said. "I'd expect these to be from Jack Dragon's Lexus."

"Sure—the Lexus was parked in the carport the morning he found her body." Fenway tilted her head. "Wait—there's just *one* set of tire tracks. Did he only park in the carport the morning of her murder?"

"It seems so," McVie said. "Although maybe the ground was dry when he picked her up before. Or perhaps he didn't drive into the carport before."

Fenway shut her eyes tight. "Hang on." There was something— something Nancy Kissamee had said. Something beyond completely ignoring Fenway. Nancy Kissamee had thought Jack Dragon had wanted to get closer to Victoria Versini—*I didn't think she was his type.* She was young and attractive; he was impeccably dressed and had a high opinion of himself—Fenway could see Jack Dragon tolerating Victoria's chattiness for a chance to get her into bed.

But if Dragon was driving Victoria, why would anyone cut the brake lines of the Alfa Romeo?

"You okay?" McVie asked.

Fenway opened her eyes. "There's something I'm not seeing—but it's got to be right in front of me."

"Maybe if you go in the house and come back out, it'll come to you."

"I guess."

Fenway followed McVie up the steps into the log cabin and ducked under the police tape across the doorway as he held it up for her.

"So," Fenway said, walking into the bedroom, "she was found in here at her computer. So she was working on something."

"And we probably won't know what that was," McVie said. "The laptop was destroyed by the shotgun blast. I hear that CSI is sending it to a recovery firm in L.A., but I wouldn't hold my breath."

"Do we think that's relevant? What she was working on?"

"Maybe she was getting ready to out her father on her Photoxio feed," McVie mused.

"Possibly—I wonder if that could have been saved to Photoxio's servers?"

McVie shrugged. "We can dig into that."

"No defensive wounds," Fenway said. "She didn't put up her hand to block the blast. Was she surprised, or did she know her attacker and didn't think they'd actually shoot her in the face?"

"Could be either."

Fenway tapped her chin. "The laptop monitor was halfway down—not closed, but not open. She had enough time to hide what she was working on. I'd suggest that it's likely she knew her attacker."

"All our suspects so far are people she knew," McVie said. "Yep Younger—she'd just done an article on him. And, of course, that letter you found in the Alfa Romeo suggests that either she had already confronted him about being her father, or she was about to."

"She didn't confront him at Diamond Hills, though," Fenway

said. "Or at least, if she did, all her tire tracks have been covered up. We need to get camera footage from ATMs, traffic lights—see where she went and if she met him."

"Phone records will help—after Christmas, though."

Fenway sighed and dropped her shoulders. "Maybe we should do what the rest of the world is doing and take tomorrow off."

"We're already here. Let's keep walking through it."

Fenway closed her eyes again. "Okay—so let's assume the shotgun is in the closet. How would the killer know it was there?"

McVie tilted his head. "Henry Rampart—and Tricia—both knew it was there."

"And Victoria knew it was there, too. So if she—" Fenway stopped and closed her eyes again.

"What is it?"

"Hold on." She pictured Victoria in her mind's eye, typing a review on her laptop, darkness falling over the cabin. "It's late," Fenway said. "Maybe eleven o'clock or midnight—and she hears a car pass on the road, then stop. But it's not in her driveway, so she doesn't pay much attention."

"Okay."

"Suddenly, there's a noise outside that *is* in the gravel driveway— and she grabs the shotgun from the closet. Maybe Henry was right; maybe the shells were in the nightstand drawer. But she loads the shotgun and goes outside to scare the intruder away."

"But she was killed *inside*."

"When she sees someone—maybe her birth father—cutting the brake lines. Maybe she threatens him with the gun and they go inside the house, where he overpowers her." Fenway opened her eyes.

"That story doesn't rule out Henry Rampart." McVie scratched his temple. "Nor, I suppose, Tricia Rampart."

"Why would she bring the killer into the bedroom?" Fenway said. "Nancy Kissamee thought Jack Dragon might be on the prowl —maybe we're wrong on the whole father thing, and Victoria brought home someone from a bar or a club and things went sideways really fast."

"But there were no other fingerprints in here," McVie said. "That suggests that the killer knew they were going to need to hide their fingerprints." He pointed at Fenway. "Your theory makes a lot of sense. Whoever cut the brake lines probably did so with gloves on because they didn't want their fingerprints on the car parts."

"So they came to the cabin intending to kill Victoria—just not intending to kill her with a shotgun."

"And, even though I've said Henry or Tricia Rampart might have done it, this story fits best with Yep Younger. The letter from Victoria's car establishes motive—she was threatening to take away his livelihood. He's connected to a couple of the zip codes and letters from the note we found in Victoria's trailer. And not only was the murder weapon found at his house, the hose cutter—with fresh brake fluid on it—was found at his place of work. I agree with you that there are questions I can't answer—"

"Why was the letter in Victoria's car? What do the other zip codes and letters in Victoria's note mean? And what was the order of events? When did Victoria's brake lines get cut?"

"Yes—all good questions. But here's another question: if Yep Younger didn't kill Victoria, who did?"

McVie's phone buzzed in his pocket, and a second later, Fenway's phone buzzed in her hand. Fenway looked at the screen; it was a text from Dez.

Yep Younger arraigned - $250,000 bail
He posted and will be released in an hour

Fenway frowned. "Only a quarter million for bail?"

McVie looked up from his phone and nodded. "I can hear the lawyer now—pillar of the community, no flight risk, owns a business at the busiest time of the year, strenuously denies allegations, the whole thing."

Fenway stared at the desk, the pellet holes still fresh. At least the splatters of blood and tissue had been cleaned up.

"I think," McVie said carefully, "we've got the killer. Maybe not as neatly as we'd like, but we have enough to convict if the ADA does his job. And once we have phone records between Victoria— and, let's hope, Yep Younger—we'll be able to establish a timeline."

"Maybe I'm overthinking it," said Fenway.

"Possibly." McVie scratched his chin. "But your gut has been right before. Let's see what else we can find here."

But carefully walking around the inside of the cabin—what there was of it—revealed very little. No evidence. No shotgun. Nothing out of place. Nothing in Victoria's suitcase to suggest why she'd spend time at the local Christmas parade of an out-of-the-way beach town. The note with the letters and zip codes and the letter Victoria had written to Yep Younger were all they had to go on to establish motive. After two hours of searching—going back outside the house, too, in the hopes that something would jog Fenway's memory—they decided to go back into town.

Fenway was quiet in the car on the way back to the sheriff's office. She kept turning over the conversation with Nancy Kissamee in her mind. Victoria had been a motormouth about her father. Was there something she'd revealed to Kissamee that Fenway had missed?

Fenway looked up as McVie turned the opposite way on Fourth Street from the station.

"Did you just turn the wrong way?"

"You look like you could use some lengua tacos," McVie said. "And Dos Milagros is open until two."

Fenway looked at McVie and smiled.

———

After McVie dropped Fenway off after lunch, she babysat her email and typed up her notes from the visit to the cabin. At four o'clock, she decided to go to the hospital to visit her father.

When she arrived at Nathaniel Ferris's room, Charlotte wasn't there. Fenway sat with him, reading another couple of chapters of the book aloud, then sitting and staring into space. Charlotte hadn't responded to the first text Fenway had sent, so Fenway called her.

Charlotte picked up on the first ring. It sounded like she was in the car.

"Fenway?"

"Hi, Charlotte—uh, merry Christmas Eve. Are we still on for tomorrow?"

"Sure," Charlotte said distractedly.

"Everything okay?"

"I just spent the day in Laguna Beach with my mother," she said. "I got a guilt trip about not staying there for Christmas." Charlotte paused. "Where are you?"

"With Dad."

"Ah. How's he doing?"

"The same."

Silence for a moment. "What time do you want to come by for dinner?"

Fenway hesitated. "You know," she said slowly, "I mentioned a couple of days ago that maybe you and I should go to the Christmas parade."

"I don't know, Fenway. It was something your father liked to do for the community. Put on a show that was better than all the other beach towns around here. There's something about it that wouldn't feel right without him there."

"I think he'd be sad if you didn't go just because he wasn't there," Fenway said. "The company still paid for the parade—he'd want the community to enjoy it. And that includes you, too."

Charlotte paused. "With everything that's happened, Fenway, I'm not sure if going to the parade is a good idea. I know I've been running some aspects of the company with your father gone—and you don't know half of the power struggles and all the underhanded stuff I've had to deal with."

"I could guess," Fenway said.

"Some of the board members think I'm Nathaniel Ferris's trophy wife," Charlotte said. "They're trying to stage a coup."

"Oh. I didn't know that." There was silence for a moment before Fenway spoke again. "Why not go somewhere your efforts will be appreciated, then? Go see the positive aspects of what Ferris Energy does for the town? Dad would want you to go."

A long sigh. "If I go, you're coming with me."

"Sure."

"And you're helping me cook dinner when we get back."

"That's fine."

"And we're having that bottle of Riesling I've been saving."

"Now you're talking."

"Okay." Charlotte exhaled long and slow. "How about I pick you up tomorrow at eight?"

Fenway was quiet for a moment.

"Ah." Charlotte chuckled. "How about I pick you up from Sheriff McVie's at eight?"

"Thanks, Charlotte."

———

"Wow." Fenway wiped her mouth with her napkin, then pushed herself back from McVie's kitchen table. "I had no idea you could make pheasant."

"I wanted to do something special," McVie said. "And I wanted to show off a little, too. Let you know you're not dating a man who's useless in the kitchen."

I'm never around long enough to find out. Fenway leaned forward, reached above her plate, and grabbed her wineglass. She took a sip.

"So how was it? I figure Maxime's is better—I'm not French,

and my oven doesn't cost as much as a sports car. But it wasn't too bad, right?"

"Fishing for compliments isn't becoming," Fenway said. "Now if I say I like it, you won't know if it's a real compliment or if I just don't want you to feel bad."

"I'll risk it."

Fenway smiled. "It was delicious. You really can't go wrong when you wrap anything in bacon." She set her wineglass down. "I shouldn't drink too much more. Charlotte's picking me up at eight tomorrow morning."

"She's picking you up?"

Fenway nodded. "We're going to the Christmas parade. She doesn't have anything to do tomorrow, and Ferris Energy paid, like, a zillion dollars to sponsor it. I figure she and I can make an appearance—I think they have box seats for us somewhere at the Christmas tree farm, so we can see all the floats as soon as they come out of the barn, or whatever."

"Sounds like you have an amazing amount of Christmas spirit."

I'm not doing too bad for it being the first Christmas without my mom. Fenway smiled sweetly. "Bah humbug."

"All right," McVie said, "so do you want to leave here at seven thirty? Or do you want more time to get ready at home?"

"She's—she's actually picking me up from here."

McVie nodded. "You're telling your family about us dating?"

"What there is of my family, yes." Fenway cleared her throat. "Okay—so what's the order? Dessert first? Or presents?"

"My folks always did dessert first. And the kids had to clean up all the dishes before we got presents."

"Sounds like they knew how to milk Christmas for all it was worth."

"It worked for us." McVie stood up from the table and walked to the fridge, pulling out a small cheesecake. "This isn't homemade —I spent all my time and effort on the pheasant—but it is from Uncle Jürgen's over on Tenth."

"You know, I've lived here nine months, and I've never had an Uncle Jürgen's cheesecake."

"That changes tonight." McVie smiled, pulling a knife out of the butcher block and cutting two pieces.

Fenway tapped her foot under the table. She was nervous—this was the first time they'd had a gift exchange since she and McVie started dating.

McVie brought the two plates of cheesecake to the table. "Do you want coffee?"

She took the cheesecake and the fork from McVie. "I won't be able to get to sleep." Fenway cut off a large bite and stuck it in her mouth.

Wow. That was delicious cheesecake.

Fenway insisted on doing the dishes after dinner, but McVie wound up doing much of the work, as he knew where everything went in his small kitchen. Her hands only slightly pruny, Fenway picked up the breadbox-sized gift from the floor next to McVie's front door and brought it with her to the sofa, sitting across from the brightly decorated tree in the corner of his living room.

"Now for the moment of truth," Fenway said, trying to put a jovial tone in her voice but feeling herself break into a sweat.

"I actually got you two gifts," McVie said.

"Two gifts?"

"I just had the one," he said, "but I saw this yesterday, and I couldn't resist." He turned and bent over to retrieve a gift from under the tree. "This first."

Fenway opened the wrapper, and a yellow book cover stared back at her. "Is this—is this *The Curious Lives of Legendary Creatures*?"

McVie grinned. "Your very own copy. I know it's the paperback, not the excruciatingly heavy hardback version, but you'll have to deal with it."

Fenway opened the book and saw a chart labeled *Winged*

Monsters—beautiful illustrations with just the right amount of whimsy. She felt a grin spread across her face. "I love it!"

"Now you won't have to pay any late fees when you don't feel like driving all the way to Paso Querido."

"You say that like it's the other side of the planet."

"Sometimes, when you've had a long day, it might as well be."

"Thank you." Fenway handed McVie's gift to him. "Your turn."

McVie's eyes went wide when he saw the cartoon spaceship and lasers on the box, along with a photo of two video game controllers. "The SonicSlate System 200?"

Fenway nodded. "Sure is."

"But—this is sold out everywhere!"

She winked at him. "You've got to know the right people." Well, her father knew the right people, and Fenway called them. That was enough. "I figured you could bribe Megan to come over more often with this. But you'll have to buy the games. If I had a house, I would have had to take out a second mortgage just on the game system."

"I can get the games—oh, wow. Thanks, Fenway." He stood. "Okay, now for your real gift. I'll be right back." He walked down the hall.

Fenway sighed. She'd lost the bet two days before—she was sure the gift would be the key to his apartment.

Fenway eyed the wineglass on the kitchen table but decided not to get up.

Most other women would want this. She was almost thirty. McVie was stable, rational, handsome—and not afraid of commitment. She *should* want this, right?

Fenway heard a light switch flick on, a closet door opening, the sound of something moving, and then McVie was back.

Carrying a painting.

It was a landscape: a hillside with a wild swath of thin-limbed trees and a firework-like burst of star-shaped blue flowers. Fenway's eyes swept from the bottom left to the top right, and she could feel the hope and the joy in the canvas.

"Those flowers are California lilacs," McVie said. "Officially 'Puget Blues.' I figured that would speak to your time in Seattle, too. You know, Puget Sound and everything."

Fenway's jaw dropped open. "Did—did my..."

McVie nodded. "Yeah, your mom painted this. Charlotte said it's about twenty-five years old. You would have been about four."

"I've never seen it before."

"Your father had it in storage. I don't know if there's a story behind it or what, but I thought it was beautiful, and I thought it should be on your wall."

"Wow," Fenway said, "I don't—"

And then her voice broke, and the tears came streaming down her face.

McVie jumped onto the sofa and took Fenway in his arms. "Oh —hey, I'm sorry, I didn't mean—"

"I just miss her so much," Fenway mumbled between sobs, burying her face in McVie's shoulder. "I don't know how I'll get through this without her." *And I'm so angry with her for letting that money disappear.* She banished the thought from her mind.

"You have people who love—who care for you here," McVie said.

"I don't know what to say to my dad," Fenway gulped.

"I get it," McVie said. "But he'll come out of it."

"You don't know that," Fenway said. "Have you ever had someone literally take a bullet for you?"

McVie didn't say anything, just held her tightly and stroked her hair.

PART 4

CHRISTMAS DAY

CHAPTER FIFTEEN

Fenway sat bolt upright in bed.

"The Mercedes SUV!"

McVie rolled over. "What?"

"The Ramparts' Mercedes SUV."

"What are you talking about?"

Fenway switched on the bedside lamp. Her copy of *The Curious Lives of Legendary Creatures* was next to the clock, which read 5:37 A.M. "When we first interviewed the Ramparts, there was a Mercedes SUV in their back driveway."

McVie grunted. "So?"

"So? A high-end SUV like that might have high-end tires on it. I can go do a DMV search. Maybe we can see if that type of Pincellani tires are on that."

"If you don't come back to bed, you'll scare Santa off."

Fenway grabbed a pair of dark blue jeans and brown boots from her bag, pulled the nightgown over her head, and put on her bra and a cream blouse.

"Are you getting dressed?"

"And we still don't have an explanation for those tires—the least

I can do is see if Yep Younger has any expensive SUVs registered in his name."

"He seems more like a ten-year-old pickup guy to me."

"Thanks for everything last night, Craig." Fenway hurried around to his side of the bed and bent down to kiss his cheek, then stopped.

"What?" McVie mumbled.

"You haven't given me your key yet."

McVie pushed himself into a sitting position and rubbed his eyes. "No."

"But I lost the bet."

"At first, I thought you were just making fun of me for being practical." McVie looked Fenway in the eyes. "But you're not ready to take that step yet."

Fenway was silent.

"If—*when*—you take my key," McVie continued, "I want you to be excited about it. I want you to do it because you want to take another step with me." He shook his head. "Not because you lost a bet."

"Thank you." Fenway kissed his cheek. "That means—that means a lot."

McVie reached out and took her hand. "*You* mean a lot."

She straightened up and cleared her throat. "Charlotte is coming to pick me up in three hours. I've got work to do." She turned to go, then rushed back to the nightstand and grabbed the book.

———

Fenway arrived at her office in the dark, turned off the alarm, and ran her hand over her face. Java Jim's was closed this early in the morning, so she docked her laptop and turned it on, then walked out to the coffee vending machine and pushed the *latte* button. After a couple of minutes, the disturbingly small paper cup was full, and she walked back to her office. Halfway there, she realized that Java Jim's wouldn't be open at all because it was Christmas Day.

She opened the DMV application and searched for *Patricia Rampart*. And sure enough, the system spit back a brand-new SUV: a Mercedes G-series 550.

She opened a browser window and searched on the Mercedes website until she found it: the G-series 550 came with Pincellani Moderna Classicos.

She opened another browser window and searched for a few moments until she discovered a photo of the tread. Fenway opened her phone and swiped until she found the picture of the tread mark in the dirt at Diamond Hill. It was a match.

She took a deep breath. It might not mean anything—there were a lot of people in Estancia who drove luxury SUVs. Especially in that area—the hills above Estancia were full of second homes for Silicon Valley millionaires and the occasional L.A. celebrity.

She opened another browser window and did what she should have done two days before: she searched for the social media pages of Victoria Versini—and Vicki Johnson, too.

Vicki Johnson was a common name, but by filtering for the ones with Estancia High connections—and with a past in Arizona—she was able to narrow it down after only twenty minutes.

It was an old social media site that had fallen out of favor, but there was Vicki Johnson: a photo of a younger Versini with a different hairstyle. Her posts were uniformly terrible: she was constantly putting the other students down, making fun of their hair or their clothes. The slut-shaming was constant, interrupted only to point out other girls' physical flaws. Fenway felt sick to her stomach as she read them. She scrolled down, getting to her senior year, and there it was: a list of everything that was wrong with Avery Rampart.

She opened a new window and searched for Avery's obituary.

Ten weeks after Victoria posted the list, Avery Rampart had taken her own life. Fenway paused, her finger poised over the mouse button. That seemed like a long time—but was the social media list just the first of many awful comments and jabs from Vicki Johnson?

Fenway thought about what McVie had said about Henry Rampart. Maybe there *was* a diary of Avery's that Henry—or Tricia —had finally brought themselves to open and read.

Fenway went back to the social media page. Photos of Victoria from her college days, some with liquor bottles clearly in the background. Maybe she was in a twelve-step program, and maybe McVie had been right: she had come to Estancia to apologize to Henry and Tricia for being so mean to Avery. And maybe something in them snapped.

Fenway pushed away from the desk, her chair rolling back slightly. She shouldn't get ahead of herself. This was all conjecture. She wasn't even sure if they'd been able to get DNA from Yep Younger. It shouldn't matter too much, though: if Yep had been the John Peluda identified in the court documents, it would give him motive to avoid paying the million dollars, whether or not he was Victoria's actual birth father.

She glanced at the clock on her screen: 7:33 A.M. Oh no—she'd been at this for nearly two hours. Charlotte was probably leaving the mansion now. She picked up the phone.

Charlotte answered on the third ring.

"Hi, Fenway. Ready?"

"I'm actually at work—can you pick me up in front of the sheriff's office?"

"At work? On Christmas?"

"Yes, well—I'm working a case. I thought I might've had a breakthrough."

"You and your father are more alike than you know."

"What?"

"Nothing—never mind. So the sheriff's office?"

"Yes." A pause. "Do I need to bring anything?"

"Like what?"

"I don't know—like, are you and I supposed to open our gifts for each other on TV?"

"I hope not. We never did that before. Your father and I just waved to the crowd when the director said the cameras were on us."

"I can do that."

Charlotte sighed. "Yes. I guess I can too."

———

At the Christmas tree farm, Charlotte pulled into the VIP parking lot and into a space in front of a sign reading *Reserved for Ferris Energy.* Fenway walked through the staging area, seeing a few of the floats in all their glory. High school kids in marching band outfits were tuning their instruments. The sun had broken through the clouds, and the breeze was cool and light.

"This is beautiful," Charlotte said. "They've really outdone themselves this year."

"It's great," Fenway said.

Charlotte cocked her head. "Have you ever watched a Christmas parade before?"

"Not live, that's for sure." Fenway looked up at a Jack-and-the-Beanstalk-themed float, with a large treelike stalk extending thirteen or fourteen feet into the air, then the top surrounded by white, cotton-like material, with two large green feet sticking down out of it.

"How did they do that?" Charlotte said.

"That's the Moreko Garden Center," Fenway said, reading the small sign next to the beanstalk.

"Ah—they always do such a good job. Family-run business, but their oldest son is a mechanical engineer in Los Angeles. He must have designed that."

"Makes me almost wish the coroner's office had done a float." She turned to Charlotte with a mischievous grin. "Red blood dripping from a green knife. It would be quite festive."

"Oh, that's disgusting."

"Instead of toe tags, we could have gift tags. *To: The Grim Reaper. From: Santa.*"

Charlotte attempted to make a disgusted face, but she stifled a laugh. "How awful."

Fenway grinned.

They arrived at a set of bleachers. At the top, the middle section of benches had been removed for a six-foot-square area with an awning-like cover in alternating red and green stripes, along with two proper chairs where the benches would normally be.

"I feel like a prom queen," Fenway said.

They climbed the stairs to the top of the bleachers. A young man in a Channel 12 jacket sported a wispy mustache and held up his hand in front of him. "Authorized personnel only."

"We're with Ferris Energy," Charlotte said. "Charlotte Ferris and Nathaniel's daughter, Fenway."

The man squinted at his clipboard. "Charlotte Ferris," he said. "I don't see a Senwee."

"Fenway," Fenway said.

"It's under Charlotte Ferris and guest," Charlotte said brusquely. "She's my guest."

"Oh—of course. Sorry, Miz Ferris."

"Quite all right."

Charlotte and Fenway walked into the small area and took the two seats. Fenway could see the starting gate of the parade, and if she craned her neck to the left, she could see most of the way down the road that led downtown.

"This is quite a good view," Charlotte said. "Better than the one we had last year."

"It's nice," Fenway said.

"It's better than the view the TV commentators get."

"Where's that?"

Charlotte pointed to a raised dais about fifty feet away from the bleachers. "It's closer, though, so maybe they can describe the costumes better."

"It's a great view."

"I wish you had something to compare it to," Charlotte said.

They sat in silence for a moment.

"How much longer until it starts?" Fenway asked.

"The TV coverage starts at eight thirty," Charlotte said, "but they talk about the history of Estancia for a few minutes, and then I think they talk about the highlights. Then the mayor comes out and declares the parade open. That usually takes about twenty minutes."

"So," Fenway said, glancing at her phone, "about an hour?"

"Give or take," Charlotte said. She took a deep breath and settled into her seat. "So tell me, how are things going?"

"Okay, I guess," Fenway said. "A murder case always takes my mind off things."

"I meant," Charlotte said, lowering her voice, "how things are going with Craig."

"Oh." Fenway shifted uncomfortably in her seat. "I guess they're going okay. It's a little weird since he won't be working with me in another week. But it'll make it less likely to have a conflict of interest with him."

Charlotte chuckled. "Whenever I ask how things are with you, you tell me about your job. I mean, how is your relationship? Does he treat you well?"

"Oh." Fenway managed a smile. "I'm not very good at relationships. I've only been in a couple that have lasted longer than a few weeks."

"I know," Charlotte said. "That's why I'm asking."

Fenway looked down at the ground, then back at Charlotte. "The painting was amazing."

"I worried that it would be too much."

Fenway shrugged. "It was, in a way, but that's okay. It's hard to think about not being with Mom at the holidays. But it was nice to have a painting of hers I'd never seen. Thank you for that."

"It was his idea. I just found one that your father hadn't put up. I think he'd be thrilled for you to have it." She looked at Fenway out of the corner of her eye. "Craig had to get it reframed. That wasn't cheap."

"I wasn't—"

"I just didn't want you to think he didn't put any effort into it."

"No, of course not." Fenway grabbed her purse from under the chair and pulled out *The Curious Lives of Legendary Creatures*. "Look what else he got me."

Charlotte's brow furrowed. "I didn't know you were into mermaids and elves."

"Well, I'm not, really. But there's been a little of it on this case, and we interviewed one of the suspect's daughters who works at the public library in P.Q., and I saw this on the shelf. I decided not to check out the book because I never go to P.Q., but then Craig bought it for me."

Charlotte nodded. "I'm glad he notices things like that about you. It's a good sign."

Fenway flipped the book open. "See, there's some cool stuff in here—I was flipping through it last night before I went to sleep. A lot of the mythical creatures are similar, but there are subtle differences in different cultures. Like how there are giants—like Jack and the Beanstalk—in dozens of different cultures. Bigfoot and Sasquatch and the Yeti—it's kind of fascinating. Unicorns and mermaids and dragons..."

Charlotte nodded. "It's not really my thing, but I'm glad that Craig was thoughtful enough to notice that you—" She tilted her head. "Fenway?"

"Dragons," Fenway muttered.

She turned pages in the book until she came to the chapter on dragons, then flipped a few pages until she found a chart.

"There's the tarasque," she mumbled. "French dragon."

She turned a page and pointed. "Look—a Vietnamese dragon with a spiral tail. Responsible for bringing rain in times of drought. It's called a—well, how about that. A 'long.'"

"A what?"

"A long."

"A long what?"

"That's what the type of dragon is called. Long." She turned back a page to the French dragons. "And—look, there's a dragon called—"

Fenway's eyes widened.

"What?" Charlotte asked.

"I don't believe it. The 'peluda.'"

Charlotte paused. "I'm sorry—is that supposed to mean something to me?"

"S-T-L," Fenway murmured, "S-T-L—oh, there it is."

"S-T-L?"

"I thought it was an abbreviation for St. Louis. But it's not. It's St. Leonard—St. Leonard's Forest Dragon, to be precise."

Charlotte squinted. "Are you okay?"

Fenway took out her phone and opened her photos to the zip code note from Victoria Versini's trailer. "I don't believe this."

"What?"

Fenway turned the screen to Charlotte.

$L - 32230$
$P - 85077$
$StL - 77104$
$K - 15248$
$D - 93415$

"L—that's for his last name. It was Michael John Long when he was growing up in Jacksonville." She shook her head. "Duval County—I should have made the connection." She blinked. "P for Peluda—we knew that was the one from Arizona, but it stands for

Peluda, not Phoenix. And StL for St. Leonard's Forest Dragon—
that's either totally stupid or insanely clever. And that's when John
Peluda left Rose Ellen Johnson for the woman in Texas..."

Charlotte gave Fenway a sad smile. "I don't have any idea what
you're talking about, Fenway. Is this about dragons, or is this about
your murder investigation?"

"It's both," Fenway said. "Sorry, Charlotte. Give me a few
minutes. I've got to make a phone call."

"It's Christmas. This can't wait?"

"I don't think it can, no."

Fenway hurried down the bleachers, tapping on her phone as
she went, her purse over her shoulder and *The Curious Lives of
Legendary Creatures* in her other hand.

She tapped McVie's name and held the phone to her ear.

"Mmm—what?"

"Craig," she said. "I think I figured it out."

"Figured what out?"

"Victoria Versini *was* searching for her father. But it wasn't Yep
Younger."

"What? But—but what about the letter from Versini? The one
stuck in her floor mat?"

"Oh—the letter!" Fenway put the phone on speaker and walked
behind the bleachers into an area where she hoped she could find
more privacy.

"Do I—do I hear a marching band?"

"Yes. Charlotte and I are at the Christmas tree farm. For the
parade."

"Oh—oh, right. I guess I should watch that."

"Hang on, Craig. Let me get to a quieter area." She walked
another twenty feet, stopping next to the television dais. The band
noise was muted here. Maybe that was the reason the parade's orga-
nizers had assembled the dais in this spot. "Is that better?"

"Much."

"The letter," Fenway repeated. She tapped on the photo. "Listen to this. The first sentence: 'Thirty-one years ago, you got a woman named Ellen Rose Johnson pregnant.' That's wrong. We should have noticed. Her name is Rose Ellen, not Ellen Rose."

"Oh. Yeah, you're right, we should have noticed."

"And further on: 'A judge in Arizona has determined that you owe my mother and me for eighteen years of child support.'"

"What's wrong with that?"

"Victoria's mother is dead. The judge determined that only *Victoria* was owed the back child support—her mother isn't mentioned in the final decision. Plus, she signed it 'Vicki.' No one has known her as 'Vicki' in a decade."

"So—hold on," McVie said. "So you're saying the note to Yep from Victoria was fake."

"That's right."

"What about the note with all the letters and zip codes?"

"I think that one is real."

He clicked his tongue. "But we haven't cracked the code yet."

Fenway grinned. "I think I have."

"Really?"

"The D on that note doesn't stand for Diamond Hill. It stands for Dragon."

"Dragon? Like Jack Dragon?"

"Arrested for car theft in Duval County—that's Jacksonville, Florida, zip code 32220—under the name *Michael John Long*. L for 'Long'—which is also the name of a kind of Vietnamese dragon."

"Sorry—what do dragons have to do with this?"

"I think," Fenway said, "that Michael John Long has been criss-crossing the country, changing his last name to different types of dragons. The letters don't stand for cities—they stand for the last name of the alias he used." Fenway shook her head. "Can't you see a nineteen-year-old boy, obsessed with dragons, finding out that his given last name is a type of dragon? He knows he has to escape his past, so he changes his name."

"Are you sure about this?"

"P is for Peluda, as in John Peluda, with a zip code in Phoenix. That's the name he used when he got Victoria's mom pregnant."

"Is 'peluda' a type of dragon?"

"Sure is—it's the Spanish term for a dragon that terrorized villages in southern France during the Middle Ages."

"Really?"

"And the 'StL'—it doesn't stand for St. Louis. It stands for St. Leonard—there's a St. Leonard's Forest Dragon in English folklore. I bet we'll find one of Dragon's aliases in the Houston area with the surname of St. Leonard."

"So—this whole dragon surname business—it makes you think he wrote the note? And that he's Victoria's birth father?"

"Correct."

"But he couldn't even get the mother's name right."

"Maybe she went by Ellen, or, I don't know—I mean, it was thirty years ago. He got her name mostly right but mixed up her first and middle names."

"I remember the names of all the women I've slept with." He took in a sharp breath. "Of course, maybe that number is significantly lower than Jack Dragon's."

Fenway shrugged even though McVie couldn't see her. "Fair enough."

"Wasn't there another one? A zip code matching with a K?"

"I haven't figured that one out yet. But when I *do* find a type of dragon that begins with K, you better believe we'll find an alias in Pittsburgh with that name."

The sound of bedclothes rustling. "Okay. I'll get to the office and get cracking on those names. But that's thin. It's certainly too thin for a conviction, let alone an indictment."

"Just connect the name 'John Peluda' to Jack Dragon. We've got his fingerprints from the cabin. We might not catch him today, but we'll get him soon enough. And this should be enough to get Yep Younger out of trouble."

"What else?"

"I don't know." Fenway shuffled her feet—then it clicked.

"Oh—when we interviewed Nancy Kissamee."

"Yeah?"

"She wasn't sure why Dragon offered Versini a ride—I kept focusing on her saying that she didn't think Victoria was his type. But it wasn't because he was hitting on her. She was dropping hints that she knew he was her father. *That's* why he offered to drive her."

"Ah, that makes sense."

"And Nancy said that Jack wanted to show off his new SUV."

McVie clicked his tongue. "She *did* say that, didn't she?"

"But what car did he have at the cabin the morning we found Victoria's body?"

"Oh," McVie said, and Fenway could almost hear the gears turning in his head. "The Lexus sedan."

"Right. Even though there were mud and dings from rocks on the bottom of the car. An SUV would have made more sense to drive."

"If he had a new SUV, why didn't he drive it?"

"You know what I think?" Fenway said, pacing next to the dais. "If we can get a warrant for his house and garage, we'll find a new luxury SUV with Victoria's blood on the driver's seat—I bet he was covered in blood after shooting her. He's had time to clean the SUV, but a little luminol should make things clear enough."

"Yeah," McVie said. "I know a judge who I hope won't mind getting a call on Christmas Day."

"I hope this doesn't make you late for dinner with Megan."

"Once I pull out the SonicSlate 200, all will be forgiven."

Fenway chuckled. "Glad I could help." She paused. "Do I need to come down to the sheriff's office?"

"Aren't you with Charlotte?"

"Yeah."

"Enjoy the parade. Jack Dragon is one of the emcees, right? He's probably still in his trailer. We've got a few deputies stationed at the Christmas tree farm. I'll call it in as soon as I hang up with you, and he'll be getting a knock on his door in less than five minutes."

"Excellent."

"You did good, Fenway."

"Thanks."

A pause. "I'm sad we won't be working together anymore."

"Yeah. Me too. Now get off the phone so you can get Jack Dragon arrested for murder."

"Will do."

Fenway ended the call and turned toward the bleachers—and ran straight into a man in a long leather overcoat with an impeccably tailored gray suit underneath.

Jack Dragon.

And he had a Blue Heron shotgun in his hand.

CHAPTER SIXTEEN

JACK DRAGON'S FACE WAS CURLED INTO A SNEER. "ARREST ME FOR murder," he said softly. "I suspected you were on the right track. I didn't think you'd work everything out until after you could get the DNA results, though—and by then I'd have liquidated my assets and been long gone."

"Mexico?" Fenway said. The word squeaked out of her.

He smiled. "Never you mind. Now march." He motioned with the Blue Heron shotgun.

"So you *are* the one who stole Yep Younger's gun." Fenway started walking toward the bleachers.

Jack Dragon shrugged. "If you're going to open your gun safe with a combination during our interview, don't be surprised if I notice what the combination is. His own fault, really." He nudged her with the barrel of the shotgun. "Not that way. Toward the trees."

Fenway veered toward the Douglas firs but tried to look for a way to get toward the crowd. The marching band music was louder, but there were trees and a barn-like building between them and any type of crowd. "You were pretty close to getting away with it."

"It was going so well when you arrested Yep Younger," Jack said. "I regret that the pull of the cameras and the praise of the crowds were too much for me. I should have killed him last night when I had the chance. A nice little suicide note confessing to the crime." He shook his head. "Where did you find that paper that Vicki wrote all the zip codes on?"

"In an old jewelry box in her trailer."

Dragon's upper lip curled. "The jewelry box. Of course."

"Are you the one who cut Victoria's brake lines, too?"

"That stupid gravel driveway," he said. "It made too much noise. And then things got a little messy."

Of course. He'd come in the middle of the night to cut Victoria's brake lines—probably dressed all in black, maybe even parking his vehicle far away. Then the next morning, he'd probably cancel on picking her up. She would never have made it down the hill alive.

"She interrupted you." Fenway dragged her feet to slow down. "She had a shotgun when she caught you cutting her brake lines. So she forced you inside to discuss terms of your payment. You wrested the shotgun away from her and killed her."

Dragon was silent.

"But you had her blood all over you," Fenway said. "I'm guessing you took your SUV that night but got blood all over the inside when you drove yourself home. A pricey SUV, for sure, but nothing too ostentatious. An Audi?"

Dragon chuckled. "A Maserati."

Fenway was wrong about the ostentatious part.

"And yes," Dragon continued, "it's true I had to drive the Lexus to the cabin the next day, but the mess in the Maz is nothing too terrible. A nice detail and wax should make everything as good as new. The floor mats, alas, couldn't be saved, and the dealership charges a fortune for replacements." He motioned with the shotgun. "Walk faster."

"I was just on the phone with the sheriff. You don't want another murder on your conscience. Or on your record. I'm a law enforcement officer. You could get the death penalty."

"Probably preferable to spending the rest of my life in a cell with an open toilet." Dragon chuckled. "I can change my plans. I'll be long gone in just few minutes."

He was probably trying to lead them to a place where a shotgun blast could be confused for a car backfiring—or maybe somewhere close to his escape vehicle, so he could kill her and make an easy getaway.

Could she try to run? Would he risk shooting her in an area where he would be more likely to get caught?

If she went where he wanted her to go, she'd be shot for sure. This way—well, she at least had a chance.

She turned her head a bit. If they could pass the building on the left, and if she yelled—

Just then, one of the marching bands started up—a loud, long opening note. It startled her.

And it startled him too. He jerked the shotgun—

And she whirled around and smacked him in the face with the book—and then grabbed the barrel of the shotgun, pushing it down, away from her.

Was that "Deck the Halls"?

"Help!" she yelled, keeping the barrel pointed down as Dragon tried to pull it up—but the marching band was so loud and obnoxious, she was sure it would drown out her voice.

She drove her body forward into his and snapped her elbow up.

It caught him in the jaw, and he fell backward.

The shotgun fired.

Fenway closed her eyes and pushed herself forward.

No pain. No burning—nothing. The shotgun had missed.

She opened her eyes just in time to get her forearm in front of her.

Her whole weight dropped onto Jack Dragon, her forearm across his neck, her knee pulled up, catching him right below the sternum.

He made a terrible gasping noise and dropped the shotgun.

The band played louder as Dragon fell onto his back, Fenway on top of him.

Dragon's hands flew to his neck, and he opened his mouth to get air. He closed his mouth and opened it again like a fish.

Fenway kicked the shotgun out of reach. She straightened her leg—pain bloomed from her kneecap.

Two uniformed deputies appeared in Fenway's peripheral vision.

"Miss Stevenson!" one of them yelled.

Fenway turned Dragon onto his belly.

The marching band started "Deck the Halls" over, or maybe it was the second verse.

"Jack Dragon," Fenway croaked, "you are under arrest for the murder of Victoria Versini. You have the right to remain silent."

One of the deputies handed Fenway a pair of handcuffs. Fenway noticed that Dragon's leather overcoat had gotten badly scuffed in the fall. Jack Dragon made a great wheezing noise, then started coughing, a harsh, grating sound.

"You okay?" Fenway said.

Dragon, coughing, nodded.

She pulled his hands behind his back, cuffing him, pain radiating from her knee. Then she raised her voice over the band to finish reading him his Miranda rights.

She rolled off him, sitting on the dusty ground, and one of the deputies hauled Dragon to his feet.

One of the deputies spoke to Fenway, but she couldn't hear him over the band. She nodded anyway.

Dragon stopped coughing, angrily shouted something incoherent, then started coughing again.

The deputies led Dragon away. The one who'd spoken with

Fenway pulled out his radio; Fenway barely heard the crackle of the static over the music.

The band played a slow, overly dramatic ending to the second verse of "Deck the Halls," and Fenway realized she was breathing fast and heavy. She exhaled long and slow, then took a deep, shuddering breath. The pounding in her ears subsided.

Fenway stood up, her knee throbbing, and dusted herself off. She'd probably need to go to the sheriff's office to make a statement —but had that opening note of "Deck the Halls" really been loud enough to drown out the shotgun blast?

She looked around. If the barrel of the gun had been pointing under her arm when Dragon fired it, the ammunition might have gone into the woods or maybe even the ground a few yards behind where she had fallen on top of him.

Hopefully the blast didn't do any damage—she'd have to check.

She searched through the trees for a few minutes, but she found nothing. She turned and went back to where the scuffle had taken place. Still, no one was around.

Fenway stood there for a moment. She scanned the dirt for twenty or thirty feet in every direction. Two shotgun shells lay several yards away from where the gun had been fired. She took out her phone and took pictures of the shells, then a longer shot of the surrounding area, and finally took an evidence bag out of her purse and turned it inside out to pick up the shells.

The deputies had taken the Blue Heron shotgun with them.

She bent down to where they'd scuffled. *The Curious Lives of Legendary Creatures* lay on the ground. The cover had a crease in it, and the edges of the pages were dusty, but the book otherwise looked undamaged.

Fenway took another deep breath and walked back toward the bleachers. Her knee felt marginally better with every step.

After convincing Charlotte to come to the parade, Fenway felt bad for leaving before it even started.

She looked up toward the bleachers. Charlotte stood at the top of the steps, a worried look on her face.

"Are you okay?" Charlotte asked. "I thought I heard a gunshot."

"Yeah," Fenway said.

"Does that mean you're okay, or that there was a gunshot?"

"Uh—both, I guess."

"You're limping."

Fenway looked down. "Bruised my knee. It's not bad."

"Do we need to leave?"

Fenway nodded, and Charlotte rushed down the steps toward her.

"You can stay here. I can take an Uber to the sheriff's office." Fenway paused. "The parade is down to one emcee."

"What?" Charlotte gasped. "Did Jack or Nancy get shot?"

"No, no. Jack is—well, he won't be available."

"What happened?" Charlotte looked at Fenway's face, then looked her up and down. "You're filthy. Have you been in a—oh. Did you catch the killer?"

Fenway nodded.

"It was Jack?"

Fenway hesitated.

"Never mind, I know you can't tell me," Charlotte said. "I'll drive you. Sheriff's office, you said?"

"You don't have to come."

"Nonsense," Charlotte said.

"I'll have to give a statement. There'll be paperwork. It'll take an hour, maybe two. Maybe more than that."

"I'm driving you," Charlotte said. "And I will wait as long as it takes. Come on." She turned and walked toward the VIP parking area, pulling her keys out of her purse.

"Then we'll go to the hospital to see Nate," Charlotte said. "And then back to the house. Dinner might be late, and it might be small, but it will be a Christmas dinner." She glanced at Fenway. "And you could probably use some wine."

"Or maybe something stronger," Fenway mumbled.

They reached the car and got in, and Fenway leaned her head against the window as Charlotte started the engine.

Last Christmas, she was reveling in the straight A's she'd gotten in her forensics classes at Seattle University. She and her mother were sitting down to a dinner of roast turkey breast and sweet potatoes, discussing what Fenway would do after getting her master's, neither of them having any idea it would be their last holiday together.

This year wasn't the Christmas Fenway wanted.

But catching a murderer—that was something.

Maybe tomorrow she'd go to a clearance sale and buy a three-foot-tall fake plastic tree. So next year wouldn't feel so empty.

She'd talk to McVie—

Oh, McVie.

She pulled her phone out, and it rang in her hand. She tapped *Answer*.

"I was just about to call you." Her voice shook.

"I heard what happened from Deputy Callahan—are you okay?" McVie asked.

"I—I'm a little dusty."

"Did you get hurt?"

"No, I'm not hurt."

"She's limping," Charlotte said loudly.

"A bruise," Fenway said quickly.

"I'm just getting in the car now," McVie said. "I'll meet you at the station."

Fenway smiled. "Yeah. Okay." She exhaled, attempting a laugh. "I didn't want to spend Christmas Day doing paperwork."

"I'll cancel on Amy."

"No way," Fenway said. "I'm having Christmas dinner with Charlotte, and I'm not canceling on her. You can't cancel. Not with Megan there."

"Are you sure?"

"But you can come over afterward."

A pause. "Yeah. I'd like that."

"You can help me hang my new painting." Fenway settled back in her seat. "It'll look good over my bed."

CAST OF CHARACTERS

Fenway Stevenson: A former nurse practitioner with a master's degree in forensics, she moved to Estancia in April after her mother lost her battle with cancer. Fenway has a rocky relationship with her father. First appointed to fill out the coroner's term, she was re-elected seven weeks ago.

Her family and friends

Nathaniel Ferris: The richest, most powerful man in the county, the oil magnate founded and owned Ferris Energy. Six weeks ago, he took a bullet for Fenway, and has been in a coma ever since.

Charlotte Ferris: Twenty-five years younger than Nathaniel, Fenway's stepmother finds herself running on fumes as she juggles the demands of running Ferris Energy while dealing with her comatose husband.

Piper Patten: Formerly in the county's IT department,

this willowy redhead is a whiz at forensic accounting and data gathering. She likes the command line interface almost as much as she likes her boyfriend, Migs.

Co-workers and law enforcement personnel

Sergeant Desirée "Dez" Roubideaux: A detective in the coroner's office, Dez has worked for the county for 25 years. She's a dedicated, determined investigator despite her wisecracks.

Sheriff Craig McVie: The sheriff of Dominguez County lost the mayoral race in November. Recently divorced from Amy, he officially started dating Fenway after the election.

Melissa de la Garza: A CSI tech from neighboring San Miguelito County, de la Garza's team is a shared forensic resource with Dominguez County.

Deputy Celeste Salvador: A sheriff's deputy and friend of Fenway's.

Miguel Castaneda: The paralegal in Fenway's office, he's getting his law degree and dating Piper.

Victims, suspects, and witnesses

Victoria Versini: A rising star of both social media and the culinary world, she is found murdered in a remote cabin.

Jack Dragon and **Nancy Kissamee**: These local television personalities have hosted the Estancia Christmas Parade for years. This Christmas, they were preparing to share the spotlight with Victoria Versini.

Henry and **Tricia Rampart**: The owners of the remote cabin, they became guardians to Victoria after her mother died when she was in high school.

Danica Punch: The put-upon personal assistant of Victoria Versini.

Kendra Chanticleer: An employee at Suncoast Dream Ranch, known for their award-winning eggplants.

Yissichar "Yep" Younger: The introverted owner of the local Diamond Hill artichoke farm.

Marla Quiñones: A manager at Diamond Hill, she's active in local Libertarian organizations.

MORE BY PAUL AUSTIN ARDOIN

The Fenway Stevenson Mysteries

Book One: The Reluctant Coroner

Book Two: The Incumbent Coroner

Book Three: The Candidate Coroner

Book Four: The Upstaged Coroner

Book Five: The Courtroom Coroner

Novella: The Christmas Coroner

Book Six: The Watchful Coroner

Book Seven: The Accused Coroner

Novella: The Clandestine Coroner

Book Eight: The Offside Coroner

Collections

Books 1–3 of The Fenway Stevenson Mysteries

Books 4-6 of The Fenway Stevenson Mysteries

The Woodhead & Becker Mysteries

Book One: The Winterstone Murder

Book Two: The Bridegroom Murder

Book Three: The Trailer Park Murder *(coming soon)*

Dez Roubideaux

Bad Weather

Sign up for *The Coroner's Report,*

Paul Austin Ardoin's fortnightly newsletter:

http://www.paulaustinardoin.com

Subscribe to Paul's Patreon, with several levels of members-only goodies:

https://www.patreon.com/paulaustinardoin

I hope you enjoyed reading this book as much as I enjoyed writing it. If you did, I'd sincerely appreciate a review on your favorite book retailer's website, Goodreads, and BookBub. Reviews are crucial for any author, and even just a line or two can make a huge difference.

ACKNOWLEDGMENTS

This book is being published on the same day I leave Sacramento to move halfway across the country. Almost five years ago, I discovered the Sacramento chapter of NaNoWriMo (National Novel Writing Month), and I finished the book that became *The Reluctant Coroner* because of the support, advice, and encouragement of the people there. For the last three years, I've been one of the MLs (municipal liaisons—basically the regional coordinators) for SacNano, and (pandemic notwithstanding) it's been wonderful. Sacramento has a vibrant writing scene that includes the Wordforge Novelists group, whose members have critiqued every Fenway novel since Book Two.

Many thanks to my editor Jess Reynolds (another SacNano'er), and to my early readers, especially Dana Luco and Max Christian Hansen (my Sacramento NaNoWriMo co-ML for three years)—and of course my mother, who has been one of the proofreaders of every one of my Fenway books. Big thanks to my cover designer Ziad Ezzat of Feral Creative. My books are much better because of you.

Thanks to my patrons, including J.W. Atkinson, Sandy D'Alene, Stan Peters, Janice Webber, and Donna White.

As I begin my new adventure as a midwesterner, I'd like to give special thanks to Cheryl Shoults, who has been invaluable creating, organizing, and maintaining the newsletter, website, reader teams, promotions, and a million other items. I'd also like to thank three other new midwesterners: my wife and kids, to whom I am deeply grateful for encouragement and support.

Made in the USA
Columbia, SC
20 December 2022

74469470R00121